Pin It on a Dead Man

A Dorothea Montgomery Mystery

by

Elizabeth Jukes

Copyright 2018 © by Elizabeth Jukes

For information, email Cozy Cat Press, cozycatpress@aol.com or visit our website at: www.cozycatpress.com

COZY CAT
P R E S S

ISBN: 978-1-946063-51-9
Printed in the United States of America

Cover design by Paula Ellenberger
www.paulaellenberger.com

10 9 8 7 6 5 4 3 2 1

To Jon, my beloved and my friend

Chapter 1: Familiar Strangers

"Arriving 10:45 a.m." announced Dorothea, looking up from the early morning telegram and peering across the breakfast table at her husband, Charles. "'Still have stray from ship.' Edith doesn't explain what she means by that."

"Typical of your sister," said Charles after swallowing the last of his coffee.

"Yes," replied Dorothea, smiling fondly. "Very mysterious."

"Right up your alley then. Are you sending Dilman to get them from the station?" From the tilt of her head Charles already knew the answer.

"Of course not!" declared Dorothea. "They've had a long journey and I want to be the first to greet them."

"And Hugh Morton?" queried Charles.

"Oh," said Dorothea her shoulders slumping ever so slightly. "I had hoped to put that off. I suppose it must be done." She stared blankly at a half eaten piece of toast spread liberally with marmalade.

"Yes," said Charles gently, getting up and kissing the top of her head, "it does. I'll try to get away from the office to greet your sister and company when you fetch them home."

After Charles left, Dorothea Montgomery continued sitting and musing at the breakfast table. She had long since recognized it as her favorite meal of the day. Many of her "diverse imaginations were imagined" and discussed at this agreeable interval. She was a petite woman just past her middle 50's. Her hair, once black, was misted with silver except for one jet patch at the nape of her neck. Her hair was rolled in the old way and not bobbed in the latest style, much to the bemused wonder of her troop of Girl Guides. Pouring herself another cup of coffee, she sighed. Charles hadn't needed to remind her about Hugh Morton; apprehension regarding the inevitable unpleasant encounter with him had left her lying awake for some time the previous night thus robbing her of the much more pleasant anticipation of reuniting with her older sister, Edith, and meeting Edith's grandchildren, George and Alice. The little group had been traveling for almost a week, first on the ship from England and then across from Halifax, Nova Scotia, to Dorothea's small town of Willowsdown in Ontario and finally arriving at their destination later this morning at 10:45.

She sighed again. *I'll just finish this coffee*, she thought, *and then I'd best face the music.*

A young woman, with a glowing crown of red-gold hair, entered the dining room and looked questioningly at Dorothea.

"Dianna, right on time as always," said Dorothea warmly.

Dianna Jones was one of the Montgomerys' housemaids. Dianna's grandmother had been lady's maid to Dorothea's mother and as such, Dianna seemed like one of the family.

"You can clear away, Dianna. I'll finish this cup and bring it to the kitchen. Now," she said, tapping the telegram, "this telegram from my sister, Edith, Mrs. Heyer, says she has 'a stray' from the ship. Knowing my sister, my guess is she's included this someone into their group, so if you could make up another room please."

"Yes, Mrs. Montgomery," said Dianna. She loaded up a tray with jam and cream and eggcups and other breakfast paraphernalia.

"I also need to speak with Gladys. Is she in the kitchen?"

"She is."

"Alright then. I'll be there momentarily."

In the kitchen, Dorothea said cheerily, "Good morning, everyone. Excellent coffee as always, Mrs. White. Mmmm, smells delicious."

"Well and I'm hoping it's as good as it smells. It's been a long while since I've cooked up a steak and kidney pie but I was thinking how's it might make them feel at home," replied Betty White, the cook for the Montgomery household. Dorothea knew it was wrong but it nonetheless gave her secret satisfaction that Mrs. White's steady, reliable character and consistently mouthwatering meals meant that Mrs. White was considered a culinary jewel. Dorothea herself, then, was looked on with some envy by many of her neighbors and … she didn't care.

"I'm sure it will," was Dorothea's sincere reply. "I've already mentioned to Dianna that we'll need another room made up because it sounds as though my sister is bringing along an extra visitor besides her grandchildren, George and Alice. Gladys, I'd like you to be certain that there are enough hot water bottles for everyone and, I think, holly arranged in vases in the bedrooms would be a nice touch."

"Yes, ma'am," answered Gladys Cooper, a new addition to the household within the last month or so. When it was only Charles and herself, Dianna was completely capable of carrying the load but with the coming visitors, Dorothea had taken on Gladys. She had so far proven herself to be a bright, careful and hardworking young woman.

Dorothea heard some mutterings from the direction of Dilman White, Betty White's husband and the Montgomerys' gardener/chauffeur/odd job man, sounding very much like "craziness allowing strangers into the house." A few years back, Dilman had had a run in with the Prohibition police but it had been sorted out satisfactorily and left Dorothea and Charles with an utterly loyal, if opinionated, employee.

Dorothea didn't comment but fixed her eye on him saying firmly, "I'll need the car before 10:30 this morning as I will be picking up our guests at the station." She emphasized the "I" because Dilman was of the opinion that, contrary to the evidence, Mrs. Montgomery was not to be trusted behind the wheel of a car especially one so wondrous as the Brooks' steam engine sedan.

"Is there holly enough for all the bedrooms, Dilman?" she asked.

"Oh, yes; that'll be right enough," replied Dilman.

"Wonderful. Well," said Dorothea, nodding at Dianna and Gladys, "I think that's all. Unless you have any questions, let's carry on with the day—the last quiet one for the foreseeable future."

She waited until the girls had left and then remarked to Betty and Dilman, "I have a dismal task ahead of me before the delightful one of meeting my sister."

"And what is that, my dear?" asked Betty, cutting butter into the scone dough.

"I have to speak with Mr. Morton about the cost of Mrs. Jones' casket."

"Morton's a grave robber before the body even gets in the grave," snorted Dilman.

When Dianna's grandmother, Mrs. Jones, who had faithfully served Dorothea's mother, died the previous week, Dorothea happily paid for the funeral expenses. Happily, that is, until she saw the casket in which Mrs.

Jones was buried. That casket was not the one in which she lay during the visitation and was certainly not the casket Dorothea had paid for.

Mr. Hugh Morton was the town of Willowsdown's funeral director. Many a rumor circulated that he overcharged clients for inferior products, such as caskets that were pine but were cleverly stained to look like oak. Or urns supposedly etched with gold but in fact only touched up with gold paint. Some people noticed and others in their emotional state did not. But Dorothea was a noticer. The casket lowered into the grave was decidedly a nicely stained pine box but not the gleaming oak casket in which Mrs. Jones lay during the visitation hours. One can hardly open a dispute at the graveside. It would seem that capitalizing on this emotional moment was how Mr. Morton had managed to bury the evidence as it were.

"He cows people," continued Dorothea, "especially since it comes down to their word against his, so no one presses for restitution. Although when Mr. Clarendon saw which urn Mr. Morton had placed his brother's ashes in, he compelled Mr. Morton to replace it with the one that had been ordered and he paid Mr. Morton only the price of the lesser valued urn."

"If a bank manager can't get value for his money, I don't know who can," declared Betty, removing the steak and kidney pie from the oven. "That looks a fair treat. At supper I'll just pop it back in for warming."

"You've done it again, my girl," said Dilman, patting Betty's shoulder.

"The thought of it will console me while I chat with Mr. Morton," smiled Dorothea wryly.

This was not what she would have chosen as an ideal time for this encounter with the funeral director. Within the hour she would be meeting her eldest sister and her sister's grandchildren. Her sister, Edith, she had not seen for 41 years and she had, of course, never met Edith's grandchildren. However, the Morton meeting could not be postponed. She'd been sure to secure an appointment as Mr. Morton had a habit of not being readily available—behavior particularly unappealing in a funeral director.

It was a crisp and sparkling December morning and the walk through Willowsdown's downtown and up the hill to the funeral home had energized her brain and stiffened her resolve. She greatly disliked confrontation, although she knew there were people who actually thrived on it. But needs must. What this man was doing was wrong and shameful and she wasn't going to stand by silently.

Arthur Poole, Mr. Morton's intimidated apprentice assured her the director was in and led her to his office.

"Mrs. Montgomery," oozed Mr. Morton, directing her to a chair in front of his desk. "How delightful."

"I think we both know this is not delightful, Mr. Morton." She smiled an inward ironic smile at his expression of surprised injury. *He's very good,* she thought. "I was more than happy to pay a good price for Mrs. Jones' funeral but I will not be defrauded. I'm looking for a refund on the casket; the difference between the price of the oak one I paid for and the pine one that was actually used."

She had been standing but now sat in the chair previously proffered.

"Mrs. Montgomery, you're a woman of much insight but none of us can know everything. Woods can look very similar and it takes a practiced eye to discern differences in the grains and colors of all the various kinds."

"I find that my most poignant memories are from childhood, don't you?" asked Dorothea, her head slightly tilted.

"Ah, oh, yes without a doubt," purred Mr. Morton having faltered only slightly in rearranging his face and tone to keep up with such a sudden change in conversational direction.

"You must have many fond memories of Mrs. Jones."

"Many," sighed Dorothea. "She emigrated with us as a young woman not much older than myself. But then," she paused as if gazing back over the expanse of ocean and time, "I have vivid and living memories of an uncle with whom I was very close."

She looked up at Mr. Morton and smiled. He nodded encouragingly.

"Yes, Uncle David. I spent many hours with him as a child and learned so much. None of it has been forgotten."

"The lessons of childhood are indelible."

"Indelible: exactly the right word. Uncle David, you see, was a master craftsman. He taught me all about wood, Mr. Morton. And as you say, the lessons of childhood are indelible."

Mr. Morton looked vaguely corpse-like as the color drained from his face and he moved stiffly from where he had been standing beside Dorothea's chair to sit behind his desk.

Dorothea stood. She knew better than to feel sorry for him but there wasn't any need to be unkind so she spoke gently when she said, "I won't insist upon cash but I will be expecting cash or check by tomorrow at the latest."

At the train station, Bill Wainfleet, the town's stationmaster, checked his pocket watch—10:43 am. He knew that Mrs. Montgomery's gentrified family was coming in on the 10:45 a.m. Not that that old class rubbish carried any weight with him. He had come over those same waters just eleven years ago and here he was a stationmaster living in the stationmaster's brick house and responsible for one of the most bustling train depots in the area. He snapped the lid shut on his watch and tucked it in his pocket. Pulling it out again, he rubbed it with a soft kerchief to shimmy up the shine looking about apparently nonchalantly before stuffing it back into its resting place. Maybe it was time for a new one.

"Ah, Mr. Wainfleet, there you are. Such a lovely day for traveling, wouldn't you say?" commented Dorothea.

"Right you are, Mrs. Montgomery. Nothing like the blue of a Canadian winter sky." He liked Mrs. Montgomery. She always called him Mr. Wainfleet rather than just plain Bill. Not that he was ashamed of that name. He knew that Bill was a famous name in one of them Charles Dickens books that everyone used to read. "The porters are right and ready for her ladyship's baggage."

"Not ladyship, Mr. Wainfleet, simply Mrs. Heyer along with Miss Alice Seyler and Mr. George Seyler and... possibly someone else."

"Right you are, Mrs. Montgomery, and there's the whistle. She's right on time," he announced proprietarily.

Watching the approaching train made Dorothea realize how much stood between herself and someone of her own flesh and blood. When at age 15, Dorothea emigrated to Canada with her parents, her older sister, Edith, was already married to Harold Heyer, an important man in banking circles, and enjoying being the new star of London society. They had always been avid letter writers—she and Edith—but time and geography and life experiences had molded each woman uniquely. How would that play out in day to day, face to face interactions? Letters revealed but they also concealed. She recognized her increasing anxiety. What if Edith and her family were not at all what she had always imagined? She wondered if the "stray" they had picked up was not, as Dilman pointed out, the only stranger? There was no turning back now. A wisp of the question, "What have I done?" filtered into her consciousness and then flitted away as the train groaned and squealed to a halt.

A porter was stepping down a young woman and behind her stood an older woman with the feminized face of Dorothea's father.

"Edith," Dorothea whispered. All the years fell away and as the woman caught her eye, Dorothea waved eagerly.

"My dear Dorothea," said Edith as she stepped forward and they firmly clasped each other's hands. "This is like a dream. I kept expecting a roadblock of some sort that would keep us from meeting again. But here we are! I'm so glad to see you! Let me present to you my granddaughter Alice, who—I can't believe how time flies—just turned 19." She turned to the slight dark haired, dark eyed young woman beside her. "George is helping sort the baggage along with our friend, Ewan MacMurray."

"The 'stray'?" asked Dorothea, tilting her head.

"Of course!" replied Edith brightly.

"Alice, I am delighted to meet you," said Dorothea, turning to Edith's granddaughter and kissing her lightly on both cheeks. "Welcome to Willowsdown."

"Thank you. I must admit I feel very far from home."

"I can imagine. I think you'll find that although there are certainly differences from dear old England, there are also many similarities. I hope it will feel homey for you very soon. And these must be our fellows."

Edith lay a hand on the arm of the taller, dark haired young man whose almost black eyes matched those of his sister's.

"George, this is, of course, your great aunt, Aunt Dorothea."

George stepped forward and shook Dorothea's hand firmly if somewhat abruptly.

"And let me present our adoptee stray, Ewan MacMurray, lately from Egypt. Many fascinating tales we've been hearing as we've shared an ocean journey and now the train trip from Halifax."

"Indeed; how interesting! You're very welcome, Mr. MacMurray," Dorothea said to a stocky fellow with a merry expression and warm brown eyes.

"Thank you. I hadn't expected to wash up on Canadian shores as a foundling," he replied amiably. "I had planned to stay with friends in Toronto but at the voyage outset they cabled the ship to report an illness. Again in Halifax the report was that the illness hadn't abated. It was then that Mrs. Heyer extended your very kind invitation allowing me to stay here."

"Did she indeed?" Dorothea glanced at her sister with raised eyebrows. Edith looked back steadily with a serene smile. "Well, you're certainly welcome for as long as you need. And now it looks as though Mr. Wainfleet has all the luggage stacked and ready to go. We'll load the smaller trunks in the sedan and he'll have the large ones sent over."

The remainder of the morning was taken up with a round of tea and scones, with Mrs. White's inestimable crabapple jelly, some unpacking and settling and then, along with the promised arrival of Charles, a light luncheon. Now Edith was finishing the last of her unpacking. Dorothea poked her head in the bedroom door.

"How goes the unpacking?" she asked.

Gladys had been sedulously folding and arranging Edith's clothes and hats and accessories. On Edith's dresser was a parade of glittering gems, part of a lifetime's collection presented to her by an adoring husband. Dorothea's eye was caught by the glitter of one piece in particular: a brooch in the shape of a beetle about the size of a large walnut ornamented with lapis lazuli, emeralds, rubies, gold and other stunning stones. She walked to the dresser and, picking up the brooch, she breathed, "Oh, Edith, this is spectacular."

"Yes, that was Harold's most recent gift. I hesitated to bring it but being apart from him for so long I decided I wanted it near me. I pinned it on one evening for dinner with the ship's captain but somehow I felt that I would be more comfortable wearing it on solid ground so I haven't worn it since. Silly I know. Now that we'll be settled again I expect to enjoy wearing it during the Christmas festivities."

"Well, you'll be the belle of the ball," asserted Dorothea, returning the brooch to its case, "because even here we're all caught up in the Pharaoh frenzy. Isn't that right, girls?"

Gladys was finishing up in Edith's room and Dianna was just passing the door with a hot water bottle.

Dianna smiled and nodded, continuing on her way. Gladys' face had a puzzled look as she watched Dianna pass but she too grinned her assent.

"You've done well here, Gladys. You and Dianna should check in with Mrs. White; I believe she has some tasks for the two of you."

Gladys bobbed and left.

Edith's brow furrowed in thought. "You know, Gladys looks vaguely familiar; I can't think why. Now don't let me sleep too long."

"No worries there. If I don't come to fetch you, Mrs. White will. She stands no disrespect to her culinary artistry. Especially since she's conjured up a steak and kidney pie."

"Don't tell me that!" exclaimed Edith. "I may never doze off."

Dorothea laughed and left Edith to settle in.

While Edith snoozed and dreamt of steak and kidney pie, Charles returned to work at his insurance company and the young people chatted comfortably together in front of a small fire in the library. Although their acquaintance was of such short duration it had flickered quickly into a warm fellowship. Dorothea was sitting with them not really engaging in the conversation but simply enjoying hearing young people chat and thinking over how interesting Ewan's life had been. During tea he had been telling them about the archaeological dig in Egypt that he and his father were attached to. He had in fact been living in Egypt for the last four years—in fact, not long after the astonishing find of King Tutankhamen's tomb in 1922. She smiled as she recalled the exchange amongst Ewan, George and Alice. Ewan had been saying that although he enjoyed the antiquities, he had "chosen to turn the Grand Tour of the old days on its head and come to the new world for inspiration." She had asked him, "So your father's studies are not yours then?"

"I must admit," said Ewan, "my fascination for the classical cultures is as fixed as anyone's these days but I guess it's balance I'm seeking."

"Well, if nothing else," George interjected, "you'll be an interesting conversationalist."

"I think more than that, George," countered Alice. "Someone who has seen much and learned much must be someone who feels much for their fellow beings."

"Thanks for the vote of confidence, Alice," laughed Ewan. "I do hope to be more than the party centerpiece."

Dorothea had asked George, "What are your aspirations for this trip?"

He had replied airily, "Oh seeing how the other half live, I suppose."

And then, Edith had snorted, which was Dorothea's favorite part of recollecting that scene. For more than anything, that snort meant that, after all, Edith was still the sister she remembered: sparkling, unconventional, adventurous, a diehard socialite, completely without pretense and unfailingly warm hearted. The ringing of the front doorbell broke into her reverie; it was the bell used by salesmen and so on, rather than the one for visitors.

Gladys was standing in the library doorway and announced, "Mrs. Montgomery, Arthur Poole, from Morton's Funeral Services, is here and would like to speak with you."

"Ah, yes, thank you, Gladys," replied Dorothea.

Coming into the front hall, Dorothea held out her hand to the serious-looking young man who took it in a firm handshake. Arthur had been apprenticing with Mr. Morton for about a year. He had always been a soft spoken, tender hearted fellow, really very suited for the funeral business but since working for Mr. Morton he somehow seemed clamped down. The lips that had curved easily into a benevolent smile were more often compressed into a straight line.

"Good morning, Arthur," said Dorothea.

"Good morning, Mrs. Montgomery," replied Arthur solemnly. "Mr. Morton sent me with this." He handed her an envelope.

"Thank you, Arthur. Tell Mr. Morton that I appreciate his promptness." Switching to a more agreeable subject she asked, "Will you and your mother be joining the Christmas festivities at the Livingstones' in a few days hence?"

Arthur shifted on his feet on the mat that protected the hard wood floor, "Not unless Mr. Morton changes his mind about going."

"I see. I'm sorry to hear that. I'm sure there would be many who would enjoy seeing you both there. Perhaps he won't stay long."

"It would be better for everyone if he didn't. Sorry, Mrs. Montgomery, I spoke out of turn."

"Not at all. We all know he's a difficult man." She looked meaningfully at the envelope in her hand.

"More than you know," Arthur replied just under his breath. "I must get back."

"Yes, I won't keep you any longer. Thank you again, Arthur, and I hope you will be able to come out to the Livingstone Christmas party."

"Good day, Mrs. Montgomery."

Closing the door behind him, Dorothea walked thoughtfully back to the cheerful chatter in the library.

The supper of steak and kidney pie had been a huge hit and now the party was enjoying after supper games and brandy or sherry. A euchre game was in full swing with Charles, Edith, Dorothea and Ewan while Alice and George frowned studiously over the chess board.

"One of our agents told me that the Merriweather sisters have again refused to buy life insurance," said Charles to Dorothea out of the habit they had of sharing all the day's events but forgetting that most in the room had no idea to whom he was referring. "He said they were indignant to be approached again so I think it best to let sleeping dogs lie. It's a shame. They'll lose everything if anything should happen to one of them."

"We simply have to be sure our Women's Institute and churches have emergency funds to help cover such situations. Not everyone can afford regular payments," said Dorothea, looking lovingly but pointedly at Charles.

This was a standing disagreement between them. He thought insurance was the answer for life's emergencies and she thought there should be more community responsibility. She also firmly pressed his slippered foot to remind him that the subject was not of general interest.

As Edith shuffled for the next round, Dorothea returned the conversation to the reality of the moment and asked Ewan, "Are these friends you will be visiting your own or those of your father's?"

Ewan took a slow sip of brandy. "Nothing like a relaxing evening of brandy and cards," he said appreciatively. "Through a long chain of events and acquaintances, they are my friends. I've never actually met them. Correspondents you know. Mrs. Heyer, since you wore that brooch on the ship that one evening I've been meaning to ask where you came across such a stunning piece?"

Finished with shuffling and dealing, Edith touched the brooch.

"It's an original piece from an archaeological dig. There's an extended story behind it making me almost nervous at times about wearing it. I would have thought working with your father you would have seen many such."

"Not quite like that," Ewan replied. "Every dig is different of course. Some digs are very small."

"You'll have to show Mary Pequegnant, Edith," said Dorothea. "She and her husband own the town's jewelry and optometrist shop."

"'Best Looking Jewels in Town' is their motto," broke in Charles. "I'll make hearts trump."

"Mary learned about gems from her father," continued Dorothea. "She has an unerring eye for style and quality. She'll be thrilled to see such a unique and rare piece."

"I wonder why it is that Fiona Clarendon turns her nose up at the inventory at Pequegnants'?" mused Charles.

"Who is Mrs. Clarendon?" enquired Edith's granddaughter, Alice, as she waited for George to move his next chess piece.

"Fiona Clarendon is the bank manager's wife," Dorothea answered. "I can only surmise it's because she doesn't think the gems there measure up to her exacting standards."

"Hmmm," said Edith, eyes twinkling. "I'll keep an eye on my collection."

"The irony," commented Charles, "is that Mrs. Clarendon will make trips out of town for a new piece when she has one of the best selections right under her nose. Not to mention Mrs. Pequegnant who is such an expert with gems."

"A prophet is never esteemed in her own town, to coin a phrase," said Ewan.

"I do think it's something like that," said Dorothea. "Fiona Clarendon can't seem to accept that someone in a small town, and maybe especially a Canadian small town, could be so accomplished. She's originally from Oxford, apparently, and I guess you could say has never really acclimatized."

"Maybe Mary Pequegnant should join one of your digs, Ewan," said George.

Alice chided her older brother, "George, you're not paying attention. I can check mate you."

"What an exciting challenge that would be!" exclaimed Dorothea. "Too bad Mary didn't know years ago that she had such a gifted eye. Remember, Charles, after her mother died, she and her father took that half world tour? She might have been the one to verify some of your pieces, Edith."

"Funny the twists in life," said Edith. "I'm sure that after all there's a reason she's here and not there. You mentioned a Christmas party earlier, Dorothea. When is that?"

"Friday, so not tomorrow evening but the next. It's one of the highlights of the year. You'll really enjoy it, Edith," said Dorothea. "The Livingstones' are our premier family, as we said in the old days. For the last few years they've opened their home for a Christmas celebration for any of the business people in the community: the butcher, the baker, candlestick maker, the banker and the stockbroker all go out to sea so to speak. It makes for a unique mix, but the good to the community is immeasurable."

"Everyone comes in their finery, some more dazzling than others—my trick—no envy or condescension though," continued Charles. "Wouldn't you say that's true?"

"I think that captures it," agreed Dorothea.

"Except maybe for this Mrs. Clarendon?" joked Ewan.

Charles chuckled. "If there are any such lurkings in her, she doesn't show it."

"Your gems should be safe then, Big G," drolled George.

"Really, George," replied Edith, " I hardly think that Willowsdown is a hub for jewelry heists."

"Well you never know what's lurking in the inner beast."

"George, stop being so tiresome and just pay attention to the game. You're no challenge at all!" reproved Alice.

Gladys was carrying out the tray of brandy and sherry glasses past the room's lowered lights, causing their dregs to glow gold and ruby.

"Here's one more," said Ewan. "I'll just take it to the kitchen myself."

"Thank you, Ewan," replied Dorothea.

Edith, Alice and George were slowly trailing upstairs. Charles, finished with locking up, found Dorothea gazing out the window to the street. Snowflakes twirled downward gently like jewelry box ballerinas. The sphere of light from the globe of the street lamp provided a temporary stage before they nestled into the grounded white blanket.

"What are you thinking?" he asked, putting his arm around her.

"I'm thankful that each of those flakes is unique and that although they fall to the ground unexamined they had a purpose simply because they are unique."

They stood quietly together reflecting on the scene, each knowing that the other was thinking of their son, Leland, who had died 12 years ago. The horrible gaping grief of the early days was long gone. They possessed memories and the hope-giving certainty that this life, this present terra firma, was not all there was; it being merely a broken reflection of something perfect and timeless. Dorothea smiled at Charles. Switching off the lamps they too headed upstairs.

Chapter 2: Beware the Jabberwock

The next day the three young people and Dorothea and Edith sauntered into the diamond December morning with Dorothea's sweet-natured Bichon Frise, Lily, who trotted happily alongside. Alice, George and Ewan were heading to the telegraph/phone exchange office and then to just wander about. Dorothea and Edith were heading to the shops.

"Our first stop will be Johnson's Grocery Emporium," said Dorothea.

"Grocery … Emporium?"

"That's what I said when I first saw the sign go up. Rather an exalted title for a place selling cabbage heads and salted pork and other everyday morsels but Mrs. Johnson is a woman of words and grand schemes so there we have it. I must admit though they supply an impressive array."

"What are her grand schemes?"

"Their son, Chamberlain, is very bright. Mrs. Johnson has plans for him to attend Oxford."

"I see. And Mr. Johnson agrees?"

"Oh yes. He adores her and will tell anyone who listens that 'certainly, yes without a doubt he married above himself.' It's very sweet."

"And this plan is something they have the means for?"

"It hardly seems possible; but they're very hard working salt-of-the-earth kind of people so it very well might be."

"Good for them."

Leaving Lily outside to wag her tail eagerly at all comers, they stepped into the warmth of the store where their eyes fell on a display of oranges piled in a citrusy pyramid.

"Perfect for the toes of Christmas stockings," approved Edith nodding to the pile.

A tall, bespectacled man smiled at them from behind the counter as he dished out sweets into small paper bags to several customers.

"Mr. Johnson, I presume," murmured Edith.

"Quite."

A rectangularly-shaped woman with bright blue eyes burst through the swinging doors that led to the back of the store.

"Oh, Mrs. Montgomery," she gasped, vigorously wiping her hands on a red gingham apron, "I'm simply aghast that I did not hearken to the tinkling of the bell. I was immoderately engrossed in the further room, arranging in my mind how to best display our recently acquired shipment of gherkin pickles. How can I aid you? Oh! This must be your sister! How ecstatic you two must be to be reunited!"

"Mrs. Johnson, it is my pleasure to introduce you to my sister, Edith Heyer."

"I've come expressly to buy some of your hand made caramels, Mrs. Johnson. Dorothea highly recommends them."

"She's too kind," murmured Mrs. Johnson with evident gratification.

"And I need a gallon of maple syrup," said Dorothea.

"Of course. Our maple syrup supply is diminishing but as I always admonish Robert, we must ensure that we have some on hand for Christmas."

"Very wise."

"Will you venture forth with the syrup in the jug or shall I dispense it into several jars?"

"The jug is perfectly fine. Thank you, Mrs. Johnson."

Mr. Johnson's customers left and Edith moved to the end of the counter with the candy display to buy her half pound of caramels.

Mrs. Johnson stopped wiping her hands on her apron and asked Dorothea, "Will your sister and her grandchildren be part of the Christmas festivities at the Livingstones' tomorrow night?"

"Yes, indeed. Edith never could resist any social gathering. And will your son, Chamberlain, take a break from his studies at Ridley College to socialize?"

"Certainly, certainly, but as you know, Mrs. Montgomery, we are hoping for great scholastic opportunities for our Chamberlain. He's always been exceptionally bright; even as a very young boy he loved studying. I don't think he'd stray from his scholastic path but too much socializing could cement a local attachment and that would not be quite the thing. Oxford is such a ways away."

In more ways than one, thought Dorothea.

At the end of the counter Edith and Mr. Johnson were chatting and the snatch of conversation Dorothea heard was, "… without a doubt married above myself."

She smiled.

"Edwina!" she exclaimed, turning to see who had clasped her arm. In full regalia of mink collar and a jauntily tipped hat stood Dorothea's friend, Edwina Quayle.

"Heavens! Have you dragged your sister out already?" asked Edwina.

A young mother pushing a perambulator had entered the store but in rearranging her baby's blankets had bumped her behind against the display of oranges causing a cascade. The poor thing was paralyzed with horror and humiliation, especially as an orange had bounced onto the baby's head startling him into strains of outrage.

Edwina swept off her expensive hat and began filling it with oranges while Dorothea led the bewildered mother and wailing baby to the back of the store.

"No harm done, no harm done," pronounced a breathless Mr. Johnson while chasing renegade oranges.

Edwina emptied the oranges from her hat onto the counter and plunked the hat, slightly askew, back onto her head.

"Now, my dear," she said to the mother, "what you need is a cup of tea. Bring your little man with you, and Thomas will drive us to my place and you can call your order in from there. Thomas will pop the perambulator over to your house later."

She blew a kiss in Edith's direction.

"We'll meet tomorrow night," she called. "Thank you, Mr. Johnson," as that worthy man held the door open with one hand while balancing oranges in his apron with the other.

Dorothea smiled at her friend's retreating back. Leave it to Edwina to nestle the startled chicks under her wing. The whole episode had happened so quickly that Mrs. Johnson was standing with an open mouth and a jug of maple syrup suspended in mid-air.

Dorothea could feel the giggles bubbling. Edith stood motionless with her paper bag of caramels clutched in her hand. Dorothea risked a glance at her. Their eyes locked and the bubble burst.

Back at home, Mrs. White was in the kitchen with the candelabra, holding it up to the light to ensure she had polished it to its brightest sheen.

"What on earth?" she exclaimed as Dorothea and Edith burst in with rosy cheeks and brimming with laughter.

Dorothea recounted the episode at the Grocery Emporium.

Mrs. White beamed at them; not because of the story, which she thought only mildly amusing, but because she knew it was the still intact sisterly bond that caused their funny bones to be so tickled.

"By the looks of your cheeks you'll be wanting a pot of hot coffee."

"Thank you, yes. That's exactly what I came in for," replied Dorothea.

"In the morning room then?"

"Please."

Stamping of feet announced that the others had returned from their ventures.

"Sounds like you should make it a big pot."

"A big pot it is."

"Whew! It's nippy out there," said George, unraveling a scarf.

"Mrs. White is brewing up a pot of coffee so help is on the way," remarked Dorothea as they all entered the morning room, a large, bright room full of windows adjacent to the kitchen.

"Where's Ewan?" asked Edith. "Still at the telegraph office?"

"No, but he'll probably return there as often as he can," grinned George. "Couple of nice dolls there." Edith rolled her eyes at her grandson. "He's having a word with Gladys; something about hot water bottles."

"Are the children not in school?" asked Alice. "We saw so many of them skating on the river."

"They're likely doing a physical culture class," said Dorothea.

"I'm reminded of the Thames the way the river runs through the town," commented Alice.

"Me too," smiled Dorothea. "There you are, Ewan," she said as the young man poked his head around the door. "We're just waiting for some hot coffee."

"Just the thing. I think I could get used to living in this Willowsdown of yours. From what I've seen this morning it seems idyllic. Fresh-faced shop keepers, frolicking children."

"Good looking girls," broke in George.

Ewan waved his hand dismissively.

"You paint a delightful picture, Ewan, but even I can't say that all is as serene as that," said Dorothea."

"I suppose human nature is the same everywhere," mused Alice, "and even in so-called idyllic settings there is that savage beast, as the phrase goes, that lurks in the human breast."

"Just what I was saying last night," put in George, thumping his chest.

"Last night you were supposed to be paying attention to our chess game," retorted Alice.

"I think it's not where people live but people themselves that cause the trouble," observed Edith reflectively. "We so often want what we do not have and are not so choosey as to how to get it."

"Well, I'm looking forward to this party, especially after our mosey downtown," said George.

"I suppose you met Olive Robertson and Elva North, our intrepid call answer workers at the exchange office," said Dorothea, grinning and tipping her head. "You might as well know that Olive is stepping out with our local blacksmith, Isaac Kingswood. As for Elva, I haven't heard anything but she's a smart miss and will give any fellow a run for his money."

"In other words, George, be warned," said Alice.

George made a wry face at his sister.

Mrs. White entered the morning room carrying a tray with steaming coffee and cups.

Ewan jumped up to take it from her saying, "That coffee smells entirely drinkable."

"Speaking of looking forward to the party brings to mind an element of the evening that won't be so pleasant," remarked Dorothea, pouring the coffee from the silver pot.

"And what is that?" asked Edith.

"The presence of Mr. Morton, the funeral director. He arrived in Willowsdown in 1919, I think, and over these years has only become increasingly disliked by the town's people."

"Yes, you told me about yesterday's meeting with him," said Edith. "And you got your money?"

"Yes, Arthur Poole, his unhappy apprentice, brought it round during your nap."

"Why is this Mr. Morton so disliked?" asked Alice.

"To put it bluntly, he cheats people—very subtly and not consistently, so as not to be so obvious. He's a glib talker and once the bereaved person realizes that the casket they paid for was not the one used, the evidence is buried and he can sweet talk them into admitting that they must have been mistaken."

"But that's terrible!" declared Alice.

Dorothea nodded.

"Maybe he won't show," said George.

"Maybe," said Dorothea, "but he's a fellow who will flaunt what can't be proven. However, let's not think about that or we'll spoil Mrs. White's 'entirely drinkable' coffee."

"Hear, hear," cried Ewan, saluting with his coffee cup.

Very early the following morning, the sky still luminesced like a black pearl, Dorothea, barely awake, was shuffling down the hall from the bathroom. As appropriate for semi-conscious musings, she was muttering from Lewis Carroll's 'Jabberwocky':

"'Twas brillig, and the slithy toves
    Did gyre and gimble in the wabe:
    All mimsy were the borogoves,
    And the …"

A muted sort of squealy-squeaky sound followed by a vacuum-gaspy sound checked her in her profundities. She smiled to herself. *People make the funniest snoring sounds* she thought. *That reminds me*, she continued to herself, *I need to tell Dilman to put out a bottle of champagne for after tonight's party.*

"… mome raths outgrabe.
    Beware the Jabberwock, my son!
    The jaws that bite, the claws that catch!
    Beware the …"

In bed again, it's entirely possible that, after dropping back to sleep, Dorothea herself made funny snoring sounds.

Chapter 3: Community Conviviality

At the Livingstone mansion, lights glowed from behind dozens of windows beckoning the party-goers to an evening of conviviality. As the guests entered the property through the wrought iron gates, the band hired for the evening could be seen through the floor-to-ceiling windows of the palm room. Those in cars or sleighs could drive up to the front steps which were shielded from the elements by a twenty-foot awning held up by ornately worked wrought iron lamp posts. Inside, the Livingstones received their guests at the foot of the carved, curving staircase. From there, guests dispersed to the billiard room or to one of two drawing rooms, depending on whether conversation or dancing was their activity of choice.

The Montgomery contingency made their way to the room where couches and chairs had been pushed against the walls and carpets removed to make room for dancing. The chandelier on its long chain dappled the polished floor with points of light.

"My feet have been positively itching to dance!" exclaimed Edith.

"Well, let's see," said Charles, scanning the room. "I see a colleague who should make a reasonable dancing partner."

"Take me to him then," grinned Edith and she and Charles moved away to let the dancing begin.

Dorothea noticed a young woman across the room and waved. To George and Alice she said, "That's Violet Hacker. I hoped she would be able to make it this evening. I think, Alice, that you and my young friend Violet may hit it off."

Violet waved back and wove her way through the groups of guests.

"Violet! I'm glad you could be here," Dorothea said warmly, clasping both of Violet's hands and squeezing her affectionately. "Is your mother here?"

"No, she was so tired and frazzled from completing orders for tonight that a quiet evening at home was all the party she needed."

Dorothea laughed. "I can imagine. Alice and George, this is Violet Hacker. George and Alice are my sister's grandchildren. My sister, as you can see, is already in the thick of things," said Dorothea, nodding in the direction of Edith and Sir William on the dance floor. "Violet and her mother are the creators of most of the headbands and hats you'll see here tonight."

"Miss Hacker, delighted," said George with eyes somewhat agog and raising Violet's hand to his lips without even realizing it. "Would you honor me with the next dance, Miss Hacker?"

"Certainly," agreed Violet. "Perhaps we can chat later," she said to Alice as she and George headed to the dance area.

"Well there goes George for the night," said Alice drolly.

Watching them go, Dorothea remarked, "She's lovely, isn't she? Violet is the perfect name for her with that shining dark hair and creamy skin. More importantly, she's a very talented young woman."

"You mentioned headbands and hats."

"Yes, she and her mother, Annie Hacker, are the town's milliners."

"Excuse me, Mrs. Montgomery."

"Elva! How lovely to see you."

A petite, somewhat plump young woman had joined Dorothea and Alice. She held out her hand to Alice who took it in a warm handshake.

"Miss Seyler, I'm Elva North. I saw you briefly yesterday at the telegraph/exchange office where I work. Would you like to join us?" She nodded in the direction of a few young people.

"Thank you. I would like that very much."

The young women took their leave of Dorothea and she, spying an empty chair, took possession of it—from here she could do her reconnaissance. Unlike her sister, Edith, who jumped headlong into any social gathering, Dorothea liked to "scan" the participants. As a "noticer," it helped her to take the temperature, so to speak, of the various interactions. For instance, she noticed Mrs. Clarendon, she who had no use for the gems at Pequegnants' Jewelry Store, intently examining Edith's brooch. In order to participate more fully in the Charleston, Edith had flung the scarf on which she'd pinned her beetle brooch over the back of a chair. Mrs. Clarendon was reaching a hand towards the brooch when, coming up behind her, her husband, the bank manager, put his arm around her waist. *Off for a dance*, thought Dorothea. *An odd couple really*, she began musing, but then spied an even odder one. There on the dance floor was Mr. Morton, the funeral director, with Myrtle Merriweather. She noted that the other dancers gave them plenty of room and, even more telling, was Myrtle's sister, Mabel, who was glowering from the sidelines.

Mabel and Myrtle Merriweather were the sisters Charles had expressed concern for during the euchre match two evenings earlier. These two sisters were making a Herculean effort to keep their family farm. The Merriweather family had farmed there for about 80 years but the war had wiped out the brawn needed to keep it producing at a profit. Neither of them wanted to take on help: hence Charles' concern that they have insurance.

Now the talk about town was that Mr. Morton had been paying court to Myrtle, and Mabel was fuming. Even from where she sat, Dorothea perceived what just might be puffs of smoke coming from Mabel's ears. Dorothea had to admit that she shared Mabel's consternation—Mr. Morton of all people! She had always considered Myrtle to be a sensible and upright person. She decided it was time to wade in. Best sit and chat with Mabel before Mabel did something rash as she was wont to do.

"I believe Charles was hoping for a dance with you," Dorothea lied as she took a seat beside Mabel who was sitting close to where Edith's scarf was draped. "Such fun to watch people dancing, isn't it? That young man partnered with Violet is my grandnephew George and my sister, Edith, is over there." She was trying to divert Mabel from the two dancers whom everyone were furtively watching.

Mabel dragged her glaring eyes from Myrtle and Mr. Morton and followed Dorothea's pointing finger. Despite herself, Mabel smiled at Edith's evident enjoyment.

"What a treat to have your sister and her family visiting," she said kindly. "Are they here for a good length of time?" The question remained unanswered as Myrtle had left the dance floor and was moving their way. "Hmph, here's Myrtle," Mabel muttered. And to Myrtle, she asked in a strangled voice, "Aren't you finishing the dance?"

"I'm winded," Myrtle replied shortly, taking a seat beside Dorothea. "It's a treat to see you, Mrs. Montgomery." Peering through the expanse of dancers to the other side of the room, she asked, "Who are those young people? Did they come with your sister?"

Standing and chatting with Elva North was Olive Robertson, who worked with Elva at the telegraph/exchange office and a rather glamorous brother and sister duo who appeared to be in at least their mid twenties.

"They," explained Dorothea, "are Chester and Eleanor Smith from Toronto. They are Olive's cousins who've been visiting for a few days. I believe they return home tomorrow."

"They look very citified," commented Mabel.

"Yes, Mabel," replied Myrtle, "but so would Olive if she lived as the heiress she is and didn't choose to work to make her own money honestly. I'm not saying her family's money wasn't come by honestly but there are whispers."

"I don't think you can make statements about where honest money comes from," replied Mabel through pursed lips.

"Mabel," said her sister tartly, "this is hardly the time and place." Turning the conversation, Myrtle continued, "I do wish Olive's father would get over his ridiculous suspicion of Isaac Kingswood's intentions and give his blessing to an engagement."

Myrtle was referring to Olive Robertson and Willowsdown's young blacksmith, Isaac Kingswood. They had been stepping out for almost a year and were keen to be married but Olive's father accused Isaac of only wanting to marry Olive for her money.

"He's a foolish man. Life can be very short," remarked Dorothea quietly. They sat silently, contemplating. The Great War had scythed through every family represented at the party.

Their sad remembrances were broken into when Violet and George trotted up, both slightly winded.

Violet dropped onto the chair draped with Edith's brooch-adorned scarf and George onto the one beside her.

"You two have been hard at the dancing," said Dorothea.

"Violet's an ace dancer."

"You're not so bad yourself," Violet said, returning the compliment. "It's just splendid to be dancing!"

"I'm off for a drink," said George. "Can I get you something, Violet? Aunt Dorothea?"

"Punch, please," said Violet.

"Nothing for me, George, but let me present you to Mabel and Myrtle Merriweather."

"Pleased to meet you," said George, bowing slightly. "May I get either of you a drink?"

Both sisters greeted him genially but declined his offer and he departed. The sisters moved to another conversing group as Edith strode up with Chester Smith.

"Dorothea, let me introduce you to Chester Smith," she said.

Dorothea extended her hand for his handshake and turned to Violet.

"This is my young friend, Violet Hacker."

"Delighted to meet you," said Chester. "I noticed you dancing. Forgive my being forward," he continued as he sat down in George's vacated seat, "but you have a stylishness about you that makes me think you must be from the city. I'm from Toronto but I've never seen you. I made a wager with myself that you're from Montreal."

Violet removed her hand from the handshake. She folded her hands together in her lap. She took a breath.

"I am from Willowsdown," she said smoothly.

"Willowsdown," he repeated. "From here then?"

"Yes."

He looked at her intently. "And why not?" he said laughing. "You simply enhance any place where you find yourself."

"Thank you, Mr. Smith, but I must confess I haven't 'found' myself any other place."

"Well, Miss Hacker, is there any way we could change that?"

"Not unless, Mr. Smith, you know of a millinery shop in Toronto that has an opening for a hat maker and seamstress."

"A career woman! Better and better ... Miss Hacker."

Violet burst out laughing.

Grinning, Chester said, "Let me introduce you to my sister, Eleanor. She's a city career girl too."

Violet studied his face. "I would like that."

Dorothea and Edith stopped their chit chat and raised their eyebrows at each other as Chester and Violet excused themselves and Chester took Violet's hand to lead her to where Eleanor was talking with Olive Robertson and Isaac Kingswood. George appeared with a punch glass in each hand. He stopped short beside his grandmother, gaping at Violet's empty chair and then at her back as she wove to the other side of the room apparently having completely forgotten the requested drink.

Disbelief all over his face, George turned to his grandmother.

"Just the thing. Thank you, George," said Edith, plucking a glass from a slightly drooping hand.

At one point in the evening, Dorothea and Charles managed one foxtrot that left them so breathless that they were forced to escape to the billiard room where there would be no chance of Edith coaxing them into another dance. Here was an altogether different atmosphere from the sparkle and pulse of the other rooms. Here conversation was intermittent and mellow and the only percussive note was the subdued click of the billiard balls. Dorothea and Charles were seated in an alcove of the room near the door to the hallway that connected the billiard room to the rest of the house. They sat in companionable silence, sipping from punch glasses and decreasing their hearts rates.

"...veneered you thieving wretch! And another thing!" One of the two voices in the hallway of which they had been vaguely aware had risen in volume and ire. "It isn't proper to be giving her such expensive jewelry. Heaven only knows where the money comes from for it!"

Not wanting to eavesdrop on what was very obviously an uncomfortable exchange, Dorothea and Charles left their seats: Charles took his place at the billiard table and Dorothea returned to the drawing room where she caught up with Edith who was plunking herself breathless into her chair and flinging her brooch-laden scarf back around her neck. Sitting in the adjoining chairs were Mary and Bertie Pequegnant.

"Mary! Bertie!" said Dorothea, "this is the first time all evening I've been able to speak with you. Edith, this is Mary and Bertie Pequegnant. They own the jewelry and optometrist shop in town."

"'The Best Looking Jewels' in town is our motto," said Bertie Pequegnant, eagerly shaking Edith's hand.

"Yes. I've heard about this place of yours and about you in particular, Mrs. Pequegnant."

"Charles was praising your eye for a good gem," explained Dorothea.

"I was well trained," said Mary Pequegnant. "My father was a jeweler and he passed on his love for beauty to me. That piece you have is stunning. An original, I expect."

Edith removed her scarf and handed it to Mary Pequegnant for closer inspection of the beetle brooch.

"Indeed," she said. "It came out of a dig in Egypt from a few years back: a gift from my husband."

Mary Pequegnant puckered her brow as she examined it.

"Oh, Mrs. Heyer, I just have to divulge to you my admiration of your energetic dancing! Oh how distressing!" The ebullient Mrs. Johnson had trod on the fringe of Edith's scarf which was trailing on the floor and pulled it from Mary Pequegnant's hand.

"Oh my, that pin is … is stupendous!" exclaimed she of the Grocery Emporium, picking up the scarf and handing it to Edith. "I have perceived that your grandchildren are thoroughly enjoying themselves. But I understood there was another fellow with you, was there not?" she asked, looking back and forth between Dorothea and Edith.

"There was, you're absolutely right, Ewan MacMurray," nodded Dorothea. "He had been planning to stay with friends in Toronto but when they fell ill, he came to us. This morning, though, he received word that his friends are well again. He left on the train this afternoon."

"Our loss then," said Mrs. Johnson graciously. "Oh! But I perceive that Chamberlain seems to be leaving! Please forgive my dashing away."

"I take it that Chamberlain is an only child," said Edith wryly, watching Mrs. Johnson eagerly pushing her way through groups of chatting people.

"Well deduced, my dear Watson," said Dorothea.

Along with Oxford hopeful, Chamberlain Johnson, Hugh Morton also took his leave. Throughout the evening thus far, Dorothea had, out of the corner of her eye, noted Mr. Morton schmoozing himself around the room, stopping to speak with most of the guests. As far as Dorothea could tell, anyone speaking with him seemed stiff and wary and the conversations were very brief. Except with Fiona Clarendon. That confabulation appeared, if not warm, at least passably relaxed. At the close of said tete-a-tete, Mr. Morton bundled on his coat and scarf and gloves and headed for the front door, leaving alongside Chamberlain Johnson. It was still quite early in the evening, plenty of time for jollification without the dampening presence of the funeral director. She imagined she wasn't the only one breathing a sigh of relief at Mr. Morton's exit. Even such gracious hosts as the Livingstones looked lighter as they returned from seeing him off. Dorothea had just finished delivering some canapés to a few of the older guests and had been pondering these things as she was returning to her chair when a tap on her shoulder made her turn to see, Nelson Goodman, the police chief.

"Chief Goodman, I was beginning to think you weren't coming. Is Mrs. Goodman here?" she asked, peeking past him.

"No, Mary is down and out again. That's why I'm late. But she'll be well again soon," he added.

Dorothea touched his arm. "I'm sure of it," she said gently.

Mary Goodman suffered from an unknown illness that allowed her days of industry where she could care for her family with love and diligence and then without warning would knock her off her feet. "For better or for worse, in sickness and in health …" Chief Goodman had once stated to Dorothea but she knew it discouraged them both.

"Looks like a good time is being had by all," he observed.

"It's been a lovely evening so far. Good will to all for the most part. Your son Nelson Jr. has been showing up the other fellows with his dancing ... very fancy foot work."

"Ay, he's light on his feet like his mother. Well, I'll be seeing you, Mrs. Montgomery," he said, absent-mindedly tugging at a non-existent forelock.

"Hello, Dorothea," said Edith as Dorothea sat down beside her and May Withrow who was married to Willowsdown's vet, Dr. Caleb Oswald Withrow. "It seems Mrs. Withrow and I have some acquaintances in common."

"Of course," said Dorothea. "You and Harold spent some time in Calcutta."

"And so it was your father who established the veterinarian college there," said Edith, continuing her conversation.

"Yes. I spent my childhood in Calcutta. England seemed a very strange place when we moved back. But my mother's recurring malaria meant we just couldn't stay. A good thing as it turned out because I wouldn't have met my husband if we had remained in India."

"So your husband, Dr. Withrow, is from the old country?"

"No, he's from here." When Mrs. Withrow had sat down to chat with Edith, she'd sat on the chair where Edith's scarf had slid into a heap. She had placed the heaped scarf in her lap and had been fingering it in a distracted way. "On his way home from the Boer War, Caleb stopped in to visit relatives. We're actually second cousins. His plan was to pursue a career in medicine on his return to Canada."

"But?"

"As he puts it, it was my love of animals and my father's impressive work at advancing veterinarian science that led him to treating four-legged patients rather than two."

"Children and animals love these two," said Dorothea, smiling. "Let me take that scarf, May, before Edith loses it. Edith, where is your handbag? Let's put the scarf away once and for all."

"Have you been home since moving to Canada?" asked Edith, obediently proffering her heavily-beaded handbag.

"Oh no," said Mrs. Withrow, handing over the scarf. "No, that's not possible."

"We could never do without them," said Dorothea smoothly. "I'm so glad the animals kept themselves well so that both of you could join in tonight."

"Me too. Caleb has been frantically busy lately what with Mr. North's cow calving triplets and various surgeries at the office. I've hardly seen him."

Charles strode up to their circle of chairs.

"Sorry to interrupt, ladies," said Charles. "I've been sent as a messenger to you, Mrs. Withrow. Dr. Withrow says he's sorry but he has to leave immediately. He's been called out to the Brown farm. I told him I'd take you home so he leaves with a lightened burden."

May Withrow laughed. "What were we just saying about animals staying well?"

Chapter 4: Beetle, Beetle, Where's the Beetle?

Dr. Caleb Withrow's emergency exit began the exodus. The guests gathered up muffs and scarves and overcoats and galoshes and decked themselves to greet the frosty night.

'Good night' and 'thanks' were called into the crystal air as people dispersed into cars or sleighs. Those who had walked were crammed into full vehicles, increasing the conviviality of the evening.

Charles drove slowly behind a line of sleighs whose bells sparkled sound.

"I wish we still had a sleigh," sighed Dorothea.

"'Hear the sleighs with the bells—
Silver bells
What a world of merriment their melody foretells!
How they tinkle, tinkle, tinkle,
In the icy air of night!
While the stars that oversprinkle
All the heavens seem to twinkle
With a crystalline delight' … What is the rest of it?"

"Never heard it," said George somewhat grumpily.

"'While the stars that oversprinkle.' That exactly expresses how the sky looks right now," said Alice.

"Edgar Allan Poe, isn't it?" asked Edith. "I haven't thought of that poem in ages."

As they neared the Brown farm, May Withrow said, "Just drop me at the end of the lane here, Mr. Montgomery. I'm feeling rather adventurous so I'm going to do something I haven't done in ages and that's help Caleb in situ."

"Your wish is my command," said Charles as he slowed the car to a halt.

A hearty good night was expressed by all, all except George that is.

Back at home, Dianna and Gladys and Dilman were piled up with cast off winter paraphernalia.

"Do you want a game of chess?" Alice asked George. "I couldn't possibly go to sleep yet." She waved her hands in the Charleston fashion.

"Don't be absurd, Al," George replied shortly.

"Alice, dear, how about some of that champagne Dilman set out and a sit down to hear about your time at the party," suggested Edith.

"Alright." Alice threw a puzzled look at her brother.

"If I know Mrs. White she'll have some sandwiches to go along with the bubbly," said Charles. "How about a go at them, eh, George?"

"Sure," said George gruffly.

"We'll leave the ladies to compare notes. Dilman will have a fire lit in the library. Electric fires are brilliant in many ways but there's nothing like a real fire on a cold night."

Dorothea took the sandwich tray from a weary looking Mrs. White who had tried to appear full of bustle but didn't fool Dorothea. "You're a treasure. We can dole out the sandwiches. You go to bed and tell the girls they can turn in too."

"What's the matter with George?" asked Alice, taking a bite out of a sandwich as the three women settled into comfy chairs in the sitting room.

"I think he's put out that Violet spent the rest of the evening with Chester Smith," replied Edith, opening the drawstring on her handbag and removing her scarf.

"Oh," said Alice. "Well, I understand they're leaving again tomorrow so the field will be open again. These sandwiches are delicious! I spent most of my time with

Olive and Elva so I didn't get a chance to chat with Violet."

A sort of whimper came from Edith.

"Edith?"

"My brooch is missing from the scarf."

"It must have just dropped off in your handbag," suggested Dorothea. "Did you rummage right to the bottom?"

"Well, maybe in my instant of panic I wasn't thorough but it isn't exactly a large bag. It's easy enough to see what is and isn't there," replied Edith a little tetchily.

From the beaded and bejeweled bag, which was about eight inches deep, Edith withdrew a powder compact, a handkerchief, two crushed feathers from her headband and some mints. She turned it upside down and shook it. Nothing.

She turned to Dorothea and Alice with a look of distressed bewilderment.

"But surely …" began Dorothea. She tried to recall when she'd last seen the brooch's beetle body twinkling in all its gold and emerald and lapis lazuli splendor.

"It must be," she said slowly, "that it caught on the chair, became unhinged and fell to the floor."

"That makes sense. I'm certain that's what's happened, Grandmama," said Alice eagerly.

"I'll call the Livingstones' right away," continued Dorothea reassuringly. "They'll be sure to find it. If it fell on the floor it may have been unknowingly kicked into a corner."

Edith brightened slightly. "Yes. Yes you could be right." Her face clouded over again. "But how could I have been so careless in the first place? What was I thinking to just leave it lying about?"

No answer was forthcoming.

After receiving the return call from Irene Livingstone, Dorothea replaced the telephone mouthpiece gently on its hook even as her stomach pitched itself into a free fall. She sat abruptly on the chair beside the telephone table. Charles strode into the hall. She looked at him bleakly and shook her head.

"It's not there. The alternative is unthinkable," she whispered.

"Unthinkable, but not impossible," replied Charles.

Chapter 5: Official Eyes

The next morning Chief Goodman decided that walking to the Montgomerys' would settle his breakfast as well as give him time to consider this improbable case. In his mind it was still a matter of a missing object not a stolen one. Likely Mrs. Heyer was so used to jewels being pinned here and there on her person that when something fell off she wouldn't pay it any heed. So it could be anywhere in the Livingstones' house. Not that he had ever had to unearth something from the tombs of the Pharaohs before but he had certainly rooted out many a popped and lost button in his time. He would ask some questions and then do a thorough ferreting about at the Livingstones'. He knew they had searched last night but the police were trained to look. Anyway fresh eyes and all that. Once that was done he would draw his conclusions.

Dilman answered his ring at the kitchen door.

"Morning, Chief."

"Morning, Dilman."

"They're expecting you."

"Fine but I wouldn't mind a cup of tea and a quick sit down. It's a goodly day but still a fair hike and the cold seeps in. Would there be a cup left in that pot, Betty?"

"There is indeed. We've not much of an appetite to be sure. You should see all that was left from breakfast; except for Master George, they just picked at their food. And I having gone and made black pudding so's they'd feel home like."

"They must be ruffled for sure then."

"Oh to be sure. Poor Mrs. Heyer is white as paste and Miss Alice keeps dribbling out tears. And Mrs. Montgomery clean forgot to thank me for the meal as she has done ever and anon. What a way for them to begin their visit!"

"Nobody's found anything then?"

"Nothing. But you never know when strangers come to town," commented Dilman darkly.

"I understood that one of their party has already left."

"Yep. That Ewan MacMurray fellow," nodded Dilman.

"When was it that he left?"

"Oh, well, he left yesterday morning," answered Betty. "And such a shame too. I think Miss Alice was a bit put out being as he seemed to be sure to be going to the party. But his friends sent word they were well again and were anxious to see him. I suppose they were who he really was coming to see so it made sense for him to head out promptly. But such a bonny fellow he was, it would have been so pleasant for Miss Alice to enjoy his company at the party."

"You've searched all the coats," continued Chief Goodman, heading off the matchmaking story of Betty's imagination.

"Don't know why, as the brooch was supposed to be on a scarf in her handbag. We all looked though," said Dilman, nodding at Dianna and Gladys.

"We looked really carefully, Chief Goodman," agreed Dianna.

"I'm sure you did. I didn't catch your name," he said, looking at Gladys.

"Gladys Cooper."

"You must be new to the household."

"About a month, sir."

"Alright then." Scraping his stool back from the table, he straightened his jacket. "It's most likely still at the Livingstones'. I'll go and talk with the Montgomerys and then head over. Thanks for the tea, Betty."

"They're in the sitting room at the front of the house," advised Dilman.

Chief Goodman nodded his bald head and trekked down the hall.

He found a sober group mindlessly stirring coffee cups. The Turkish carpet on the floor seemed brighter than usual against the dull looking faces sitting above it.

"Chief Goodman, thank you for coming," said Charles, rising and shaking hands.

"Coffee?" asked Dorothea, holding up the silver pot.

"No thanks. Betty just gave me a cup of tea." He got out his pad of paper. "First let me say, Mrs. Heyer, that I'm sorry this has happened. We'll find it though. It can't be far."

"That's very kind of you."

"When was the last time that you saw the brooch?"

Edith inhaled and puckered her brow.

"I showed it to Mary Pequegnant. While she was looking at it, Mrs. Johnson accidently stepped on the scarf and it fell. But it was still on the scarf because she commented on it. After that, I have to admit that I don't remember seeing it."

"Anyone else?"

There was a pause.

"Violet Hacker and I sat near the scarf," began George, "but come to think of it, I can't say I saw the brooch itself."

"Did you wear your scarf and brooch anywhere else in the house? Upstairs for example?"

Edith pondered. "I can only admit again how careless I've been because once I flung it off to dance I went upstairs only once and know for a certainty I was not wearing it."

"What was the last thing you did with the scarf?"

"I was chatting with … sorry I can't think of her name …"

"May Withrow," said Dorothea.

"Of course, from Calcutta. I was chatting with May Withrow and she was holding the scarf on her lap."

"Why was that?"

"It had been lying on the chair. She picked it up so as not it sit on it. It was then that Dorothea suggested putting it in my handbag which I did."

"And the brooch was on it?" Chief Goodman glanced between the sisters.

They looked at each other.

"It must have been," said Dorothea.

"But did you see it?"

"No," they replied in unison.

"What about either of you?" he asked of Alice and Charles.

"Early in the evening I noticed Grandmama's scarf and brooch only from a distance. The scarf, with the brooch, was hanging over the back of a chair."

"Must say I didn't notice it at all," said Charles. "Once I find my comfy corner I don't venture far. Except for one dance with Dorothea, I kept pretty much an old boys' club evening."

"Right," said Chief Goodman, pushing his hands against his knees and standing up. "Joe North and Nelson Jr. are meeting me at the Livingstones' and we'll do a thorough going over. Will stop by later when we find it."

At home Chief Goodman groaned and slumped into a chair.

"It wasn't there, Mary, as sure as shootin'. We looked under chairs and carpets and into vases and cutlery drawers, which was a bit far fetched; we looked into every nook and cranny until our eyes were popping out of our heads. It wasn't there."

He still couldn't believe it. The sheer volume of work ahead of him weighed on him but more was the bewildering distress that someone from this town could be guilty of theft.

"Who in Willowsdown would do such a thing?" asked his wife, Mary.

He shook his head and shook it again.

"An outsider?" ventured Mary.

"I hate to say it but I hope so."

Heaving himself from his chair, he said, "I need to go over to the Montgomerys' place and give them the bad news."

Chapter 6: Who Did the Dastardly Deed?

"Edith. Edith," Dorothea repeated gently.

"I'm sorry. What did you say?"

"Nothing. I was wondering though if you wanted to cable Harold or would you prefer that Charles do it for you?"

"No, I'll do it. A walk to the exchange office will likely do me some good."

"Did I hear you say something about a walk?" asked George who'd sauntered into the sitting room.

"We're going to the exchange office so your Grandmama can send a cable to your grandfather."

"Mind if I join you?" George crushed his cigarette into the ashtray on the roll top desk. "I need to clear my head."

Passing the library, Dorothea poked in her head. Alice was looking moodily into a small fire.

"Hello, dear. Would you like to walk downtown?"

Alice rose from her chair. "Yes, I think I would. Maybe Olive and Elva have heard something helpful at the exchange office."

On the way downtown George nonchalantly said, "I was thinking of dropping by Violet's digs; see where she works."

"Just come with us, George, and then we'll all go with you. I'd like to see the shop too," said Alice.

"Righto."

At the telegraph/phone exchange office, Elva North and Olive Robertson were busy at the switchboard. With their headsets on they looked like they were plugged into a giant electronic porcupine and a very busy porcupine at that with all of the pulling and pushing of cords for calls. They both nodded and smiled at the group upon their entry.

The telegram delivery boy was at loose ends at the moment so he offered to, "Do the job for 'em as he could take down a cable just as good as he could deliver 'em."

The unhappy message was sent. There was a lull in the communication world; Elva and Olive took off their headsets.

"Mrs. Heyer, I'm so sorry to hear about your brooch. My brother, Joe, helped Chief Goodman and his son with the search," said Elva.

"Thank you."

"Have you heard anything more?" asked Alice, addressing both Elva and Olive.

"Not yet," replied Elva. "But it's early days still. The news won't have got around too far quite yet."

"But I can assure you it won't be long," said Olive, smiling wryly.

"And then we'll know more than we want to know," agreed Elva, nodding her bobbed blonde head at the switchboard.

"There is one odd thing we know though…" began Olive when both switchboards lit up and the girls plugged themselves back into the porcupine.

The group pulled on their gloves, waved, and set out down the street.

"I wonder what it is they know," mused Alice.

Annie's Millinery Creations was Dorothea's favorite shop. Every hat had hidden within it a small sachet of lavender so a moment at Annie's undid hours of unrest carried from somewhere else. Perhaps too it was because it was a place of creativity that added to its atmosphere—a creativity born out of crushing grief. Annie's husband had died in debt and the war had taken both her sons. Violet's childhood sweetheart had been listed as Missing in Action, and Violet had pined for him for several years. It was eight years since the guns in Europe had been silenced and nine since Annie's Millinery Creations had opened. People said that the bleeding in theirs hearts turned to beauty in their hands. They had scrimped and saved and the debt had finally been released. For Annie, the creation of hats had acted as a comforting balm as it had for Violet for awhile. Now though, Violet was restless and longing for wider horizons for her talent and ambition. Besides that, she wanted to wear beautiful clothes to jazzy parties and never have to stay up late tacking feathers and sequins on hats destined for the flappers who seemed to have money to buy anything they wanted.

No one was around when they set the bell to tinkling and stepped in.

"I say," said George removing his hat.

"They're brilliant," breathed Alice, slowing turning around to take in all the extraordinary workmanship in the shop.

"Hello!" called Dorothea.

There was a sniffing sound and the clatter of a teacup and saucer from the back room.

"Sounds to me like Dorothea," a voice said.

The curtain dividing the workroom from the store twitched and parted revealing Edwina Quayle, Dorothea's friend and rescuer of moms and babes from cascading oranges.

"I thought it was you," said Edwina complacently.

"What are you doing back there?" asked Dorothea.

"Edith, Alice, George, delightful to see you again! How can I help you?"

Dorothea laughed. "Edwina, my dear, what are you doing here; pretending to be a shopkeeper? Where are Annie and Violet?"

"Ah, yes, well, that's why I'm here. Let's all sit down. George gather those chairs together. In fact I'm going to make an executive decision and close the store. Alice please turn over the *Open* sign. If anyone wonders why they'll know soon enough. There now."

The three who did not know Edwina obeyed silently with openly surprised faces. Dorothea, knowing Edwina, obeyed smilingly and calmly until Edwina opened her mouth.

"Violet has left," she announced.

Dorothea's smile vanished.

"Violet has left? What do you mean?"

"She went to Toronto early this morning with the Smiths—Olive's cousins."

"With the Smiths!" blurted George.

Dorothea heard a movement behind her. There was Annie with a calm face but with eyes swollen from crying.

"Annie. What is this about Violet?"

Tears glistened instantly. Dorothea rose and embraced her.

"I'm sorry, I'm sorry how foolish of me," said Annie.

"Not at all, my dear friend. Come and sit down."

George got up from his chair and motioned for Annie to sit down. She sat down composedly, crossed her ankles and held tightly to the crumpled and damp handkerchief in her hand.

"This is so unlike Violet. What did she say? How did she explain herself?" asked Dorothea.

"She arrived home late last night, well, early this morning and tiptoed into my room. Seeing I was awake she poured out, 'I know you'll be so happy to hear that

I've made some new friends, friends with connections to new ventures, better chances, something so much bigger than Willowsdown. I've been invited to Toronto over Christmas! They'll introduce me to stores where I can get a job making more money and which offer more opportunities. All of a sudden it's happened! They're Olive's cousins so you needn't worry; they really aren't strangers. But we leave tomorrow, well, today, so I have to pack. Isn't it wonderful?' And that was that."

Annie uncrossed and re-crossed her ankles.

"This morning there wasn't a chance to talk further. Eleanor Smith drove over to collect Violet so I met her. I suppose you saw her at the party?"

Dorothea and the others nodded.

"I, I guess she's perfectly fine," continued Annie. "Very smart looking, very chic, everything Violet has been eager to be a part of. She took leave of me lovingly but it was so sudden."

Annie sighed and continued.

"She's worked so hard. She deserves a change, only—" She paused and re-crossed her ankles. "I only hope," she said, her voice soft, "that her father's extravagances aren't hers."

She looked at Dorothea with earnest meaning. It had been her husband's careless and extravagant spending that had, at his death, left Annie with a burden of debt.

"You do such beautiful work," said Alice kindly.

Annie smiled at her through her tears.

"I hope you will spend Christmas with us. Will you?" asked Dorothea, squeezing Annie's hand.

Annie squeezed back. "I would like that."

Edwina saw Dorothea and company to the door.

"I'll stay with her for a bit or take her to my place," she said.

"Edwina, there's something you should know and you might as well hear it from me. The brooch that

Edith wore last night which was admired by all and sundry has gone missing—but not lost." She raised her eyebrows meaningfully.

Edwina stared at her blankly. "You don't think...?"

"No," said Dorothea firmly. "I won't think it."

Returning to their wintry walk, Edith said, "I suppose Violet's departure was the 'one odd thing' Elva and Olive knew."

"Olive would have known from her cousins," agreed Dorothea.

What Dorothea wanted to do was to march into the exchange office and intensely interrogate Olive as to the character of her cousins but she doubted that would produce any desirable results.

"I just need to stop in here," said Dorothea as they approached the Grocery Emporium. "Who's coming with me?" she asked.

The glowing interior lights revealed clumps of middle-aged women in various stages of shopping.

"Think I'll keep on—might hit the exchange again," voiced George while Edith and Alice indicated they'd accompany her.

Hardly were they in the door when Mrs. Johnson bounded out from behind the counter.

"Oh Mrs. Heyer! This is dreadful! Dreadful! I was mortified when I heard the news! Mortified! Who would do such a dastardly deed? Although I did note that Mr. Morton left early. It's impossible, quite impossible! "

"Improbable but not impossible, evidently," smiled Edith.

"Nelson Jr. Goodman had advanced to our home this morning to inquire of Chamberlain as to his desires regarding a skate on the pond. Chamberlain not abiding at home at that precise moment, and taking note of

Nelson Jr.'s fatigued appearance, I naturally solicited information as to why he looked so. He finally unburdened himself regarding the midnight oil burning expedition of scouring for your brooch."

"Chamberlain hasn't returned to Ridley has he?" asked Dorothea.

"Oh no! No, he is at rest for Christmas vacation. He must be overwhelmingly exhausted though because, as you remember, last night he left the party prematurely. If you're here about the goose and partridge for Christmas dinner, Mrs. Montgomery, they'll be delivered fresh to Mrs. White on the 23rd ready for her to work her magic."

"You read my mind, Mrs. Johnson. I will let Mrs. White know. I won't take up any more of your time," she said, nodding towards the counter where Mr. Johnson was red-faced with exerting himself on behalf of half a dozen customers.

Chapter 7: It's Not the Locals

"Stopped in to find out if Violet was the 'thing they knew' and it was," said George, ambling into the library which was fast becoming Alice's favorite room. "Elva mentioned that you and she were batting around the idea of a book club."

"Yes," replied Alice. She had been deliberating over the chess board. "I told her I belonged to one at home and wondered if there was one here. There isn't but she loved the idea and we thought we'd organize one."

"You didn't tell me."

"Well, first of all there hasn't been the opportunity: it hasn't exactly been my first thought since Grandmama's beetle business. And secondly a book club requires reading a book."

"Oh beat it," said George, lighting a cigarette.

"We thought maybe *The Great Gatsby*," continued Alice, ignoring her brother's comment.

"Could work. Saw Gladys leave the exchange office as I was approaching. Been here only a few days and already I can ankle it to the shops and see familiar faces. I think this visit will be alright."

"How magnanimous of you. You do realize that anyone who would be involved in the reading club was likely at the party and therefore a suspect in stealing Grandmama's brooch … including you."

"Me?"

"Well, you were sitting right next to it. And … you do have some debts, have you not?" Alice waved a pawn at him.

"My dear girl, if I had wanted to steal Grandmama's brooch I could have done it long before now."

"True but such a number of people allows for a greater chance that it can't be pinned on you; or anyone I suppose for that matter."

"Pun not intended I suppose."

"Very funny."

"It wasn't me; I wouldn't know where to cash in on it and anyway my debts aren't that outrageous."

"I thought you owed Ewan money from when you were playing cards on the ship."

"Well, there is that. He cleared out sooner than I expected but I'll wire him some money." He tapped cigarette ash into a jade ashtray. "Were you disappointed that he didn't stay for the party?"

Alice screwed up her face and asked, "Was it that obvious? Yes, I was disappointed at first. I like him. I would have enjoyed his company."

They sat in easy silence, George making attempts at smoke rings.

"Ewan's departure though has made me think more seriously about what I was considering before we left England," began Alice.

"There's no reason you couldn't do it. You'd be up with the best of them."

"Thanks," said Alice quietly, just a little surprised at her brother's unadulterated encouragement. "What do you think of all this?" she abruptly asked, reverting to their original subject.

"Beats me," said George, shrugging his shoulders. "We don't know anything about these people or what their motives might be."

"Nooo," replied Alice thoughtfully.

"Do you know something?"

"I'm not sure."

"I guess Goodman's the man to talk to."

"Not yet."

"Not yet? What are you waiting for? I rather think Big G would like her piece back."

"I don't want to make false accusations. It's not conclusive."

"Always the balanced thinker, eh? It's the job of the police to sort that out."

"I think I may pass it by Aunt Dorothea first; she does know these people."

"Whatever you think. Do you want to play chess or just twiddle with the pieces?"

"Play by all means. But be warned, I've been dreaming up new strategies."

George snorted. "I'll take my chances."

Nelson Goodman accelerated the police vehicle through the snow that drifted languorously across the lane to the Merriweather farm. He was making his rounds of questioning starting with those who lived outside the town and working inwards. The stone house wasn't visible from the road, hidden as it was by a row of towering pines acting as a troop of sentries. As he drew near, he could see that the wide porch was hung with Christmas swags on either side of the steps and the door was adorned with a massive wreath. The frosty breeze sighed and whispered through the pines as he mounted the porch steps but that was the only sound. He remembered when the place bustled with busy people. In 1914 both Mabel and Myrtle had enthusiastically waved off fiancées at the train station certain they would beat the enemy forthwith and be home for Christmas dinner. Mabel's fiancée was killed before Christmas; Myrtle's fiancé did come home after the Armistice but died of TB within six months. The war also claimed the lives of their two brothers, a cousin and an uncle all who had worked on the farm.

Neither sister wanted to take on help: somehow it was
expiation for the sacrifice their men made. But it meant
that the farm produced much less and was therefore
much less profitable.

"Why Chief Goodman what a surprise! Come in,"
said Mabel Merriweather brightly.

"Sorry to intrude," he said, removing his galoshes.
"Been an unpleasant development since the party last
evening."

"An unpleasant development?" questioned Myrtle,
coming into the room.

"Yes. Mrs. Montgomery's sister, Mrs. Heyer, is
missing the brooch she wore last night. It seems it may
have been stolen."

"No!" exclaimed Mabel.

"Just trying to piece together when it was last seen
so I need to ask you some questions." He pulled a small
pad of paper and a pencil from his jacket pocket. "Do
you remember seeing Mrs. Heyer's brooch?"

"Why yes," replied Mabel, "we were sitting right
next to the chair that the scarf was hanging over. Well
you were sitting next to it, Myrtle. I was one seat over."

"Is that right Myrtle?" asked the chief."

"I … I really couldn't say. I didn't notice," said
Myrtle.

"Didn't notice! How could you not? It was sparkling
there plain as day," exclaimed Mabel.

"Was there anyone else with you?"

"We were chatting with Mrs. Montgomery."

"Did anyone come near the scarf while you were
there?"

"Yes," said Myrtle quickly. "Violet sat on the very
chair with the scarf and Mrs. Montgomery's young
relative, George, sat beside her."

"About what time would you say that was?"

"Oh," mused Mabel, "maybe around 10:00 pm."

The chief looked questioningly at Myrtle.

"I suppose that's right."

"So you remember seeing the brooch, Mabel."

"Absolutely."

"But you're not sure, Myrtle."

"Well, now that I think about it, I think it must have been there. I had been dancing with Mr. Morton, you see." She kept her eyes fixed on Chief Goodman's face and didn't look at her sister. "Yes, I'm sure it was."

"How long did Violet and young George stay in those chairs?"

"George got up again very quickly. He went to get drinks," said Myrtle.

"And Violet?"

"Violet was still there but we left too," explained Mabel.

"I see. And was there any other time in the evening that you noticed the brooch?"

The sisters pondered then both shook their heads.

"After that, we were each in another part of the house and didn't see Mrs. Heyer again," explained Mabel.

"Thank you, ladies."

Chief Goodman pocketed his pad of paper and moved towards his galoshes.

"Oh you must have something to eat. It's nearly dinner time," offered Myrtle.

"On duty and have to keep going but thanks all the same."

"Well, at least take this biscuit. I'll put some jam on it," Mabel said, busying herself at the ice box.

"Obliged." He stuffed the waxed paper wrapped biscuit into his pocket, pulled his hat firmly onto his head, nodded and took his leave.

"Is your husband in, Mrs. Withrow?"

Chief Goodman stood inside the door of the vet's small waiting room.

"No but he thought he should be back early in the afternoon. Do you need him?"

"Not his professional services. I have some questions concerning the party last evening but I can start with you. In fact it's likely you can tell me more anyway."

"About the party?"

"A brooch of Mrs. Heyer's is missing, possibly stolen. I'm trying to narrow down the time it was last seen. I understand you chatted with Mrs. Heyer."

"Yes. Yes, I believe I did," she replied vaguely.

"May I sit down? Makes taking notes much easier," he commented pleasantly.

"Of course. I don't know that I can tell you anything though. We talked generally of Calcutta. I grew up there, you know, and Mrs. Heyer had also lived there for a few years so we reminisced about people and places we both knew."

"The brooch in question is shaped as a beetle inlaid with precious stones. Do you remember seeing it at any time in the evening?"

"I can't say that I do."

"When you and Mrs. Heyer were talking, did you notice it then?"

"No. Not at all."

"Do you remember picking up a scarf as you sat down?"

She paused, thinking back. "I suppose I might have."

"But you aren't sure."

"No, I'm not. I guess I was distracted by being able to talk with someone about India." She plucked at the well-worn sleeve of her cherry red cardigan.

"What time was that?"

"I think around 11:30 p.m. Yes, I'm sure because I had glanced at my watch and was so pleased that Caleb had actually been able to enjoy a leisurely evening."

"Although in the end he was called away if I remember correctly."

"Yes, to the Brown farm."

"And did you go with him?"

"No, I left with the Montgomerys but had them drop me off at the Browns."

"I see. Well, thank you, Mrs. Withrow. I think that's all for now. Please let Dr. Withrow know I may stop in to see him later."

"Unless there are animals involved, Caleb is even less likely to take note of his surroundings than I am. He probably won't be of much help to your investigation."

"Maybe not but it's worth picking as many brains as possible. Good afternoon. Thanks for your time."

By the time he reached home that night, Chief Goodman had only a handful of people left to be interviewed. But one thing was for sure. The good folk of Willowsdown were certain that no one from their town would go around stealing brooches. Well, no one, it seemed, except Mr. Morton whose name came up more than once as someone who wouldn't think twice about stealing since, as everyone knew, he was swindling people at the graveside.

Chapter 8: An Invigorating Interlude

"I've had many an adventure but this may top them all," said Edith grimacing.

She and Alice were perched on a log beside Willowsdown's frozen waterway, the Willowsbank River. Dorothea tugged fiercely at the laces of Edith's skates while Alice wrestled determinedly with hers.

The snowfall of the previous night had left a skimming easily dashed off by a concert of shovels manned by Charles and Dilman and other energetic neighbors. The town's youth scorned such useless activity and quilted the ice with their blades leaving crisscross patterns that almost negated the need for snow removal. But Sunday afternoons saw skaters of all ages and stages so the ice was regularly cleared no matter how useless the effort appeared.

"It's like riding a bike," said Dorothea. "Once you learn you never forget."

"It's not the forgetting I'm worried about; it's the learning," retorted Edith.

"Come on, Big G," said George. "I'll take you out."

"I do so dislike that nickname," said Edith to Dorothea under her breath.

To George, she said, "Alright, dear, I think I'm ready."

George in his schooling had had the opportunity to learn to skate. So far Alice had not. On the ice her ankles buckled and she felt entirely like a spindly newly birthed foal albeit a frozen one.

"I'll help you, Alice," offered Elva who had just skated up. Elva faced Alice and, holding both her hands, slowly skated backward.

"Remember you're sliding not stepping," she counseled.

Dorothea took hold of Edith's left arm and George her right, standing with her while she got her bearings. In the distance, Dorothea could see dozens of the youngest children playing tag. Some of the older girls were spinning and twirling ... and tipping over. The clear afternoon amplified the thwack of hockey stick against puck and the furious scrape of blades as boys sped toward the all-important black disc.

"That's it," encouraged Dorothea as Edith tottered forward.

Dianna Jones, Dorothea's housemaid, and her sister, Alma, skated past, chattering cheerily, leaving wisps of crystallized breath behind them. Olive Robertson and Isaac Kingswood swept past. Isaac turned and, skating backward, called out, "Good afternoon, Mrs. Montgomery. Are the blades sharp enough?"

"They seem just right. Thank you, Isaac."

He nodded and swiveled to catch up with Olive.

"Whoops!" Edith's feet did a destabilizing shuffle before righting themselves. "That was close."

"First time on skates, Mrs. Heyer?" Fiona Clarendon, skating up beside George, slowed her pace to match Dorothea and company.

"Yes, as a matter of fact," replied Edith.

"You're actually doing really well, Big G," encouraged George.

"I must say I am rather pleased with myself," replied Edith.

"Once you learn, you never forget," observed Mrs. Clarendon.

"So I've heard," said Edith."

"Has your brooch been found?" asked Mrs. Clarendon.

"Not as yet," replied Dorothea as Edith was concentrating on her feet.

"It might be quite close to home," said Mrs. Clarendon with a sideways glance across George and Edith to Dorothea.

"Oh?" queried Dorothea cautiously.

"It occurred to me that of anyone in Willowsdown, Mary Pequegnant is really the only one who would know how valuable such a piece is."

Dorothea could feel herself bristling and her breath coming with more staccato than usual.

"It's also possible that it's in fact simply lost," she asserted, a shade sharply. She didn't actually believe that but she also couldn't believe that a fellow townsperson was openly making such a slanderous accusation!

"Don't look at your feet, Big G; look ahead to where you want to go," advised George.

"That's always tremendously good advice, George, and can be applied in many situations." Dorothea looked pointedly at Mrs. Clarendon.

Mrs. Clarendon laughed, saying, "No need to get ruffled. It's only a discreet observation in the ear of those to whom it means the most. I'll leave it with you. Cheerio!" she called as she glided away.

"Well!" huffed Dorothea.

"There's always one in the crowd, my dear," said her older sister calmly.

"It could be observed," said George, "that if Mrs. Clarendon suspects Mrs. P of knowing the brooch's value, she herself must assume its value as well."

"Well observed, grandson o' mine," declared Edith.

"Grandmama! Here I am already skating on my own!" called Alice as she and Elva made to pass them.

"I haven't fallen yet." Whereupon her skates touched at the toes and she pitched forward to her knees. Pushing her tam out of her eyes, she looked up sheepishly. "I guess I can't both skate and talk yet."

"I'll be your rescuer," announced George.

"Is that so? Elva and I were doing nicely on our own, thank you very much. But you may join us just so that I can see Elva beat you in a race."

George skeptically took in Elva's slightly plump but diminutive frame.

"Go on, George," prompted Edith. "I'm doing perfectly fine."

As the young people skated away, Edith asked, "Is Elva that quick?"

"She was raised skating with her brothers. George may win only because his legs are so long but either way she'll make him work for any victory he achieves."

"It's good for him to be knocked down a peg every so often," said Edith sagely but fondly. "I hope she wins."

A short while later, Dorothea noticed that Elva had roped in Joe North, one of her brothers, making it a three-way dash—Elva, Joe and George. By now, she and Edith were moving along mostly smoothly. Alice skated up to them, with just the tiniest wobble.

"Grandmama, George asked that you and Aunt Dorothea be the judges at the finish line. We laid Elva's scarf on the ice there." She waved toward a distant spot. "I'm going to skate with them, not with any hopes of winning, of course; it's just that any competition helps me to improve at new ventures."

"The apple doesn't fall far from the tree," said Dorothea teasingly to Edith.

"No, indeed," replied a gratified Edith.

Dorothea and Edith took their place at the finish line and Alice shouted, "Go!"

During the dash, Edith asked, "Is there any possibility that Mary Pequegnant took my brooch?"

"None," Dorothea replied stoutly. "None at all."

"And others in town?"

"No. I just don't see it. Well ..."

"Yes?"

"Maybe Mr. Morton."

George, Elva and Joe swept past them; George was only a handbreadth ahead of Elva and Joe with Alice determinedly bringing up the rear.

By now the afternoon had whiled away. Dorothea and Edith were back sitting on the log removing their skates. The sky was turning topaz and simultaneously all skaters on the pond realized how cold and hungry they were.

"I'll be making up some cocoa then?" asked Mrs. White coming up to Dorothea. She and Dilman had already re-booted and with their skates dangling over Dilman's shoulder were heading back to the house.

"That would be perfect," replied Dorothea, slipping her frozen feet into chilled galoshes. "We're right behind you."

"That was fun," groaned Edith.

"It's not over yet. Not until you have unraveled from your layers and are thawing with a cup of Mrs. White's cocoa have you experienced the fullness of an afternoon of skating.

"Well lead on," said Edith.

Chapter 9: Sharing Burdens

By mid-morning on Monday, Chief Goodman was down to his last interview. Well, second to the last. He was putting from his mind the inevitable encounter with Mr. Morton. He lifted the bronze handle of the Clarendons' door knocker and looked into the blank eyes of the Pharaoh head to which the handle was attached.

"Maybe you could tell me where this blasted brooch is," he muttered.

The door was opened by Mr. Clarendon himself. Clarence Clarendon was the town's bank manager. Later in life he had married a considerably younger woman. Fiona Clarendon—Plowden as she was then—had quite charmed him with her to-the-manor-born manners. He had worked himself up from "humble beginnings", was extremely successful and respected and not a man to be crossed in business. But as much as he savored the youthful energy of Canada, he was secretly a lover of all things English country house. When Fiona, newly arrived from England, was introduced to him with her Oxford accent and high society ways, he fell headlong. He had hoped to build a home in the country and play the English squire but Fiona wanted an up-to-date house and as he could deny her nothing, they lived in Willowsdown's only modern home. Hence, the Pharaoh-shaped knocker.

"Chief Goodman. To what do I owe the honor?"

"It's a case of a stolen brooch. A brooch of considerable value."

"I had heard something of the sort. How can I help you?"

"Just trying to get an idea of when it was last seen. You and Mrs. Clarendon are the only ones from the Livingstone party I haven't talked to. I'll just need a few minutes."

Clarence Clarendon stepped back from the doorway and motioned the chief in.

"Make yourself comfortable in here, Chief Goodman, and I'll bring Fiona along."

Chief Goodman sat himself down in a white chair encircled with wood. The armrests, if they could be called that, were as high as the chair back which made him feel crunched and claustrophobic. He wasn't sure he could make himself comfortable in this room.

Mr. Clarendon returned with his wife and carrying his overcoat.

"Here we are, Chief. I'm expected back at the bank so if you could begin with me. A stolen brooch you say."

"It belongs to Mrs. Montgomery's sister, Mrs. Heyer. It's shaped as a beetle and set with valuable gems. I understand it's from an archaeological dig."

"Which dig?" questioned Mrs. Clarendon.

"Couldn't tell you. Somewhere in Egypt."

"I met Mrs. Heyer early in the evening but didn't notice a brooch," said Mr. Clarendon.

"Did you see her later in the evening?"

Mr. Clarendon frowned slightly as he recollected. "No. I spent most of the night playing billiards."

"Thank you. That's all I need for now, Mr. Clarendon."

"I'll be off then. Good luck with the investigation, Chief."

He strode over to where Fiona was sitting, shrugged on his overcoat, squeezed one of her hands, and left.

"What time was it that you last noticed Mrs. Heyer's brooch, Mrs. Clarendon?" asked the chief with pencil poised over pad.

She smiled. "Did I say I had seen it?"

Chief Goodman waited for an answer.

"It briefly caught my eye when Clarence and I were introduced to Mrs. Heyer."

"That was early in the evening."

"Yes, as Clarence said."

"And later?"

"I think I saw it out of the corner of my eye when her scarf was draped over a chair."

"Can you give me an idea of the time?"

"Nooo, no, I really can't. There were other people sitting in the vicinity as I recall. Mabel Merriweather was there and later Mrs. Montgomery and Myrtle. And I believe Violet Hacker was there at one point too. They might remember the time."

"Thanks, Mrs. Clarendon. It seems you have a good eye for faces."

Mrs. Clarendon didn't answer but reached for a cigarette box and picking one, lit it and exhaled, commenting: "It's fascinating that Mrs. Heyer's brooch came from a dig. But who in Willowsdown would know the value of such a piece? Well, besides Mrs. Pequegnant, I suppose," she finished archly.

"Can't answer that. I'll be on my way. I can show myself out."

Back on the street, Chief Goodman almost felt like wiping his brow.

At Dorothea's house, Dorothea glanced up from reading Dorothy Sayers' new mystery and gazed through the French doors of the morning room at the birds busy at the feeder, their colors or black markings distinctive against the snow. Beside her on the chair's armrest was a plate of cinnamon toast. Ever since her nursery days she'd loved cinnamon toast. There was something so consoling about it. She found it particularly soothing when she needed to contemplate any number of perplexities. If she wanted this tasty treat she always took it upon herself to go to the kitchen and create it. The toast had to be a certain toastiness and the butter needed to be spread right to the edges and then the cinnamon and sugar had to be of the right ratio and also needed to be sprinkled generously to the far reaches of the toast. And then it must be cut into four even squares. No one but herself truly had the knack for cinnamon toast perfection. Now with one square down, she was ruminating on the theft of Edith's brooch.

It has to be for money, she thought. *It isn't as though someone stole it because they wanted to possess its beauty: no one in this town would ever be able to wear it. Someone out of desperation for money has taken it to turn into cash. But who and how?* Yesterday she had told Edith that she couldn't see the possibility of anyone except Mr. Morton taking the brooch and yet here she was questioning that certainty.

"Aunt Dorothea?"

Alice was standing in the doorway.

"May I come in?"

"Of course, my dear. You never need ask."

"It's just that you looked so engrossed."

"Indeed I was, but I welcome unengrossment if there's such a word."

Alice laughed lightly and sat down. She looked through the glass at the flitting birds.

They sat silently.

"I have something to say and I'm not sure I want to share it with Chief Goodman," said Alice finally, still looking steadily outside.

"To do with the brooch theft?"

"I want to pass it by you because you know the people of this town and can tell me whether or not you think I'm reading too much into it."

"A tall order."

Alice inhaled deeply and then began, "At the party I most often found myself in the company of Olive Robertson and Isaac Kingswood. I had seen George and Violet dancing and then move off to that cluster of chairs where Grandmama had left her scarf. Just as George and Violet were heading there, Isaac excused himself and also went to that side of the room. I was only vaguely looking in that direction because I was talking to Olive but I have a hazy memory of Isaac passing behind George and Violet as they sat down. When he returned he was fidgeting with the pocket in the lining of his suit jacket. I'm sure it can't mean anything. It's just that … I have heard how Mr. Robertson views Isaac; that he's not rich enough for Olive."

Dorothea sighed.

"You've heard correctly."

"As you've heard, I have nothing tangible to share; only a supposition that may get an innocent man into trouble."

The birds had had their fill. Dorothea contemplated the now empty feeder.

She said slowly, "Chief Goodman will have enough sifting of evidence, or the lack thereof, in the next days and weeks. We'll share the burden for now and hope that nothing tangible emerges."

Edwina popped by to share lunch with Dorothea, Edith and Alice.

"No, no," she said, waving aside the cream puffs. "I've sworn off desserts. I'm 'reaching for a Lucky Strike instead of a sweet' as the jingle goes. Did you hear Dr. Payne is under the weather? 'Extremely ill' said Mrs. Payne. And … there better not be an epidemic amongst the local animals because only Dr. COW's assistant is around."

"Who is Dr. Cow?" asked Alice, laughing.

Dorothea passed an ashtray to Edwina and said, "Edwina's slipped into the local jargon. Dr. COW is an affectionate nickname for Dr. Withrow, the vet. His name is Caleb Oswald Withrow."

"Ah," said Edith and Alice together, the light dawning.

"Where are Caleb and May?" asked Dorothea.

"No one knows," Edwina replied. "He just locked up the office and put a sign on the door saying to get in touch with his assistant for any emergencies. It says he'll be back on Wednesday."

"I don't think I've ever known him to do that," stated Dorothea.

"No, always very conscientious is our Dr. COW … Withrow. The timing is a little odd, don't you think?"

"Edwina, don't you start. That kind of talk is going to spread like gangrene."

Edwina sighed. "You're right, of course. But don't tell me that the thought didn't enter your head as soon as I mentioned their absence. I saw your eyes flicker."

Dorothea tilted her head. "I have no idea what you mean," she said blinking ingenuously.

Chapter 10: The Talk of the Town

"And I have a bonny pot roast all set for supper," announced Mrs. White later that afternoon.

"Perfect," Dorothea replied. "Alice and George have gone out so it will only be Edith and me for tea. I think we'll take it in the morning room."

When the tea tray had been delivered, Dorothea and Edith settled their chairs to gaze out the windows and follow the antics of the birds. Edith took a sip from her teacup and left it cradled between her hands.

"I need to unburden myself," she announced to Dorothea.

"Unburden yourself? Heavens."

"Yes." She took another sip. "Your Mrs. White certainly knows how to make a cup of tea. The brooch is one of a pair. The archaeological research reveals that they evidently were worn, one on each shoulder. I just wear it as a brooch, of course. Harold took such trouble to track it down. He had seen a photo of it somewhere and knew I would love it." She set the cup in the saucer. "I'm sorry. I'm not relating this well. Let me start again.

"The banking world, of course, provides Harold with many opportunities to know about large sums of money or precious gems etc. that need safekeeping. Several years ago, a man met with Harold in order to open a safety deposit box in which to keep what is now my scarab brooch. I think his name was Bertram Somers or Somerville or something or other. At the time, he also showed Harold a photograph of the two brooches together, presumably taken at the excavation site. He conveyed to Harold that the second brooch had been lost shortly after the time of the photograph with no trace of it to be found. The pair of brooches had been discovered and documented early in 1923. In 1924, when he met with Harold, the second brooch was still missing. About a year ago, this man died. For ten months the brooch lay in the safety deposit box with no one claiming it. Harold had it appraised, purchased it and presented it to me. The assumption, as I understand it, is that the other brooch has long been considered to have been irrevocably lost in the sands of Egypt." She paused in her narrative.

"But ..." prompted Dorothea.

"But I have always had a faint niggling fear. What if it was stolen and not lost? The notion has always been easily cast aside because who would steal the one and not the other? Now though I wonder again. It was that qualm that made me doubt about bringing the brooch so far, and now I fear I should have listened to myself."

"Edith, I think you can safely put that to rest. No one here would know there was a matching brooch so the theft can have nothing to do with that."

"Of course. Yes, of course. This really has put me in a dither."

"It's put us all in a dither. You have lost something precious and we of Willowsdown are eyeing each other suspiciously."

Edith left the room to find a book and Dorothea admitted to herself that she didn't like the direction her thoughts were taking. She knew she couldn't be the only one in town who was "wondering" about who could have taken the brooch—forming possible scenarios of nefarious schemes by her fellow townspeople.

"Mrs. Montgomery, may I have a word?" asked Gladys who had tapped on the doorframe. Dorothea was glad to be interrupted in her bleak cogitations.

"Certainly, my dear."

"I need to give my notice. I must return home after Christmas. My mother is very ill." Gladys tumbled the words out.

Surprised, Dorothea turned in her chair to look more fully at Gladys. "I'm very sorry to hear this on both accounts. Should you leave for home sooner?"

"No. I won't be needed until after Christmas. One of my sisters is getting married then and will no longer be able to help at home."

"I see." Dorothea paused, trying to read Gladys' face. Despite her breathless announcement, her face was smooth and told Dorothea nothing. "Well, we'll miss you; you have done good work here. I was so impressed with how you calmly took care of Ewan when he had his bit of a spasm about the mixed up hot water bottles ... our mini mystery."

They both laughed at the memory.

"Well," said Dorothea, still taken aback, "if you hear differently from home, be sure to let me know, otherwise we'll proceed with the plan for you to leave after Christmas."

"Thank you, Mrs. Montgomery. I'm sorry that it's so sudden."

"Well illness can't be dictated to," replied Dorothea graciously.

As Gladys left, Edith returned with her book. Settling in her chair, she commented, "I wish I could figure out why Gladys looks familiar."

"Hey, girls, got any extra biscuits?"

Alice and George had walked into the exchange office while Elva and Olive were taking a tea break.

"Biscuits? What do you mean?" asked Elva. "We have cookies."

"Is that what you call them?"

"Biscuits are something entirely different."

George shrugged his shoulders.

"By the way, a telegram just came through for you," said Elva, picking it up to hand to him.

"Feel free to read it."

"Received the money—stop—thanks—stop—Ewan."

"Good."

"When and where would you like to first meet for our Readers' Club?" Alice asked Elva and Olive.

"How about Thursday evening at my place?" offered Olive.

"Yes, that would be fine with me," replied Alice.

"Me as well," said Elva.

"George?" asked Alice.

"The bees knees."

Alice rolled her eyes.

"What's the talk of the town today?" asked George.

Elva and Olive looked at each other.

"Ah, Grandmama's pin," said Alice.

"Including a whole lot of talk I'd rather not hear," said Olive vexedly.

"Why is that?" asked Alice.

Olive not answering, Elva glanced at her friend and said quietly, "Before we connect calls, comments are made about Olive's cousins."

"Your cousins?" George asked Olive. "You mean Eleanor and Chester Smith?"

"Yes. Comments insinuating that they took the brooch," retorted Olive her peachy skin flushed with outrage.

"Why would they?" asked Alice pointedly.

"That's just it! They wouldn't. They have no need to steal to get such jewelry and Eleanor doesn't even like Egyptian styling."

"And her brother is financially independent?" queried Alice. "I ask not out of suspicion but out of confirmation," she added as she saw Olive's hazel eyes turn icy.

"Yes, I do know that." Olive relaxed her shoulders. "I'm sorry to be so prickly. And yes, Chester is very solvent so it's all so ridiculous!"

"But not only that ..." continued Elva.

"I suppose your friend Violet is targeted as well," intervened George.

"Yes," they said together.

"People are actually saying that she took the brooch?" asked Alice.

"Again, not overtly," replied Elva.

"The whole concept of innocence until proven guilty isn't standing up too well then," commented George.

"Not too well, no," said Elva dryly.

The switchboard lit up and Elva and Olive returned to the afternoon's talk of the town.

That evening Dorothea's guests stayed in while she and Charles donned their Girl Guide and Scout leader's uniforms respectively. Charles strode to the community hall to encourage his Scouts to "Be Prepared" while Dorothea walked briskly in the biting evening air to meet Edwina at the church basement where they gave leadership to a group of 11-year-old Girl Guides. A few other people were tramping through the snow on their way to somewhere. She was surprised to see Mabel Merriweather in town. She waved as Mabel crossed the street to head up the hill towards the school and funeral home but Mabel seemed not to see her. *Must be some do at the school*, she mused. Chamberlain Johnson and

Nelson Goodman Jr., Chief Goodman's son, were trotting up the hill too but they also didn't see her. As she passed alongside the river, the open water at the bottom of the dam reflected the silver disc of the moon. She paused to gaze at it wishing that such brilliant illumination would shed light on the dark tangle of what she had started calling the bejeweled beetle business.

What light did she have? Never mind suppositions and suspicions. What facts were clear? She knew she hadn't taken the pin, nor Charles, nor Alice nor George. Her own household staff were in the clear, of course. Well, she was quite sure they were. And ... and that was all she knew. Alice and George had shared their conversation with Olive and Elva so she knew that Olive was fiercely against any accusation lodged against her cousins. But could they really know that? And Violet. She had been very restless lately. She loved beautiful things but couldn't possibly afford them. And she had been practically sitting on the brooch. And she left Willowsdown abruptly with a jet-setting brother and sister. And where were the Withrows? And what did Isaac Kingswood have in his pocket at the party if anything? Oh she hated this! Here she was back to the distasteful suspicious thoughts.

"Dorothea! Halloo!" Edwina was waving at her from the other side of the bridge. "Heavens, woman, what were you thinking about? I've been waving madly for five minutes."

Dorothea smiled at her friend's exuberant take on reality.

"Do you have the paper for the parcel wrapping? I have good news!" Edwina exclaimed without waiting for an answer to the parcel wrapping question.

"The Withrows haven't left town because they absconded with Edith's brooch."

Dorothea laughed. "So that *is* what you were thinking while you were eying the cream puffs the other day!"

"And so were you!"

"Well, yes. It may have crossed my mind, I'm very sorry to say."

"Hmph! I bet it more than crossed your mind."

"Edwina! You don't think I'm that suspicious do you?"

"Well, not suspicious; that's too negative, but certainly inquisitive and quick to put two and two together."

"Hmm. Well, what's the good news?"

"It seems Dr. Withrow received a small inheritance from some distant dead uncle and they are treating themselves to a few days away."

"Wonderful! They absolutely deserve it." Dorothea almost felt like crying she was so relieved. *And that,* she told herself, *will be the story for everyone in town.* There will be a completely logical and healthy explanation for everyone's seemingly odd behaviors.

"So did you bring the paper?" asked Edwina as they stepped into the darkened church building.

For the past few weeks, Dorothea and Edwina had been helping their Girl Guides to craft six-inch cloth dolls. Each doll looked like the intrepid Guide who had created her. The dolls, in all their glory, had been completed last week and tonight's task was for each girl to write a note to her pen pal and enclose her look-alike doll. The girls were clustered in groups of threes and fours, and during the note writing all was quiet but for scratching pens. Now there was much chatter and crackling of paper as the parcels were packaged.

"And then she said that Chamberlain said he wouldn't have to worry about money anymore," said Lottie Fletcher whose eldest sister Amelia had her name linked with Oxford hopeful Chamberlain Johnson, much to his mother's chagrin.

"Why?" asked Dora Thayler.

"I don't know. He wouldn't tell 'Melia."

"My mom said that brooch that was stolen was worth buckets of money," offered Nancy Campbell.

"Well, I think it's daft to want to go to school so far away," blurted Irene Martin.

"What does that have to do with money?" asked Dora.

"Oxford is a very prestigious school. One doesn't attend there without paying proper monetary dues," replied Millie Malone coolly.

"Really, Millie, do you have to use such fancy words? You sound just like Mrs. Johnson," said Lottie, which caused giggles all around.

Dorothea thought it best to divert the conversation before someone started drawing imaginary and possibly damaging conclusions—including herself. She recalled Mrs. Johnson's comment that Chamberlain had left the Livingstone party unaccountably early. And then she also recalled to herself her very recent resolution that odd behaviors needed the assumption of innocence rather than guilt.

"It's lovely to hear you all laughing," she said.

Infinitesimal pause, sidelong glances and more giggles.

"I think Chamberlain wants to marry Amelia," announced Nancy.

"I never said any such thing," retorted Lottie.

"Well, whether he does or he doesn't won't help you get your parcels posted to your pen pals. The dolls are delightful so let's get them wrapped up and sent to your overseas friends."

"Yes, Mrs. Montgomery," chorused the little group. All chatter subsided as they conscientiously completed the task at hand. Within twenty minutes, fourteen brown paper packages were lined up to be relinquished to the mysterious forces of airmail, and the girls trooped out into the frosty air to walk each other home.

Chapter 11: More Talk for the Town

The next morning, Dorothea heard the unexpected sound of the French doors in the morning room being opened. She was outside refilling the bird feeders with seed and suet.

"Oh my dear Mrs. Montgomery!" gasped Mrs. White. "Mr. M. wants you to phone him back immediately! It's urgent he says."

"He phoned? Is he ill?" asked Dorothea with alarm, clasping the suet cage closed and marching to the doors.

"No, no. He said it was a shocking thing and you must call him."

Dorothea stepped into the warm house.

"Here, my dear, I'll take your coat and things. You get to the phone."

"Thank you, Mrs. White."

Dorothea's voice shook as she asked to be connected to Charles' office.

Once on the line, Charles stated without preamble, "Hugh Morton has been murdered."

Mrs. White's "bonny pot roast" from the previous day made a repeat performance as a hearty and consoling stew for the noon meal; although it's likely no one actually tasted it.

"Describe this to me again, Charles," urged Dorothea.

"Morton was found this morning, in his back work room, by his apprentice Arthur Poole. He was in a closed casket with another casket leaning on top of it.

He had a spot on the side of his head where the skin was broken. Looks like he was hit on the head, presumably to render him unconscious, pushed into the casket and the other one propped so as to keep the lid closed, causing suffocation."

"Oh dear," exhaled Dorothea, slowly folding her table napkin again and again.

"'Oh dear'?" prompted Charles.

"Last evening on my way to Guides, I saw Mabel Merriweather walking up the hill. Well, striding would be a better word. You know Mabel. I thought she was going to the school but maybe she was making for the funeral home."

"Why would she?" asked Alice.

Dorothea and Charles exchanged glances.

"Mr. Morton has recently been paying court to Mabel's sister, Myrtle," began Dorothea.

"And?" said Edith.

"Mabel thinks he's a 'thieving wretch,' and actually told him so to his face," continued Dorothea.

"How do you know this?" queried George.

"Charles and I overheard part of a heated conversation between Mabel and Mr. Morton at the Livingstones' party. It was when we were recovering in the billiard room from the foxtrot. They were in the hallway. It seems he has given Myrtle some expensive jewelry."

Charles carried on, "Mabel is known for her fierce anger and impetuous actions, particularly if she perceives an injustice. She's always broken-hearted and penitent afterwards, but by then damage has been done."

Dorothea considered. "What if Mabel thought Mr. Morton had stolen your brooch, Edith, to give to Myrtle and went to confront him?"

"We'll have to tell Chief Goodman what we heard," remarked Charles regretfully.

"Not yet. Surely not yet," pleaded Dorothea. "He *was* a thieving wretch."

"Dorothea, that's beside the point," replied Charles firmly. "A man's life has been taken, wretch or no."

"I don't think the overheard snippet of a conversation should be considered as useful evidence," asserted Dorothea.

"It's always difficult to know the exact context of such an exchange," offered Alice.

"Context is everything," agreed Edith. "Conversations can have many layers."

"I think they're on to something," mumbled George while lighting a cigarette.

Charles contemplated his companions. "Valkyries," he finally said, laughing.

"I'm assuming theft and murder aren't the usual fare in Willowsdown," commented Edith after dinner when Charles had returned to work and Alice and George had gone skating.

"It's staggering," replied Dorothea, shaking her head. "As I said, Mr. Morton was an unpleasant man but still ..."

"You referred to him as more than 'unpleasant'."

"True. Our own Mrs. Jones' casket controversy was an example of his crooked business dealings so I think 'thieving wretch' is still apt. I wonder how long he's been giving Myrtle jewelry? Do you still want Mary Pequegnant to take a look at your handbag?"

"I see how your mind is working my dear, Dottie. Yes, let's jaunt down to the shops."

"Good afternoon, Mary," said Dorothea as she and Edith entered into the jewelry side of the jewelry/optometrist business.

"'Best looking jewels in town' indeed," commented Edith. "You have a exquisite selection here, Mrs. Pequegnant."

"Thank you. And your piece of jewelry… ?"

"No news," replied Edith.

"I'm sorry to hear that. I understand it was given with much love."

"Yes," said Edith, blinking against tears. Rallying she continued, "But its loss doesn't compare to today's news."

"Mr. Morton, yes. Downtown has been positively jumping. Everyone wants to talk about it. I've been very busy. Chamberlain Johnson was in looking at necklaces for his mother. And Isaac Kingswood was also studying certain gems but then many others were in not looking for anything at all; rather they just wanted an outlet to discuss the Mr. Morton situation."

"Was Isaac looking at any one gem in particular?" asked Dorothea with apparent innocence.

"Yes, as a matter of fact," replied Mary Pequegnant with a knowing look.

"Did Mr. Morton come in often?" asked Dorothea.

"Never. We've never had dealings with him. My parents, and Bertie's too, were gone before Mr. Morton took over the funeral home and there's been no other family member who has needed his services. Poor Chief Goodman: your brooch, Mrs. Heyer, and now murder for heaven's sake! I can't imagine anyone who would do either. But," she said, returning to business, "is there something I can do for you ladies?"

"I hope so," said Edith, handing over a handbag. "This is the bag that I took to the Livingstone party and it seems to be missing some of its beads and paste gems. I was wondering if you would have something with which to replace them." Mary Pequegnant held it up to the light.

"It's quite heavy—isn't it?—with all that beadwork. Yes, I think we definitely have something that will fit the bill. Do you need it again soon?"

"No, not at all; anytime after Christmas will be fine."

As she was filling out the repair label, Mary Pequegnant mused, "I've heard that Mr. Morton was paying attention to Myrtle Merriweather and giving her jewelry. But your question, Dorothea, about him coming into our shop has me wondering: if he wasn't buying from us, where was he getting the jewelry?"

"Alright, out with it," insisted Edith as, having accomplished various other errands, they tramped home.

"I'm doing it again!" said Dorothea. "I'm jumping to conclusions."

"Such as …"

"Such as if Mr. Morton wasn't buying jewelry from Pequegnants, maybe he was stealing it and maybe he did steal your brooch. I wonder if Chief Goodman has searched his place. But then on the other hand, Isaac Kingswood is looking at diamonds."

"You're assuming he was looking at diamonds. Mrs. Pequegnant didn't exactly specify. And even if he was, so what?"

"So … Olive's father will not give his blessing to an engagement between them because Isaac is not wealthy enough. Olive told me once about the first time they saw each other. Elva had suggested that Olive take her weathervane sketch to the young blacksmith who had recently taken over the town's forging business. When she peeked into the shop, she could see a strong arm beating out a copper sheet to the booming of the cannons in Tchaikovsky's *1812 Overture*. She said that his Victrola was perched on a shelf and it was the task of his assistant to turn it on and off as needed. Seeing a smartly dressed young woman peering, and then stepping into the shop, so jolted the assistant that he scraped the record with the needle. That was two years ago, and as far as I know, Mr. Robertson still considers that Isaac loves the heiress and not the person. He's evidently waiting for Isaac to present him with the evidence of a substantially lined bank account."

"Was the record ruined?"

Dorothea stopped in her tracks and stared at her sister. "The record?"

Edith looked back at her teasingly. "You're taking this far too seriously. There is nothing substantial to connect Mr. Morton or young Kingswood with my brooch."

Dorothea began walking again, shifting her parcels to the other arm. "You're right. I'm getting out of hand."

"Let's forget all about this and prepare ourselves for a rousing game of Mahjong this evening."

"That would be the cat's pajamas." Dorothea grinned. "George would be impressed with me for such up-to-date talk. I wonder … do you think Mr. Morton might have been blackmailing someone?" she mused. She glanced sideways at her sister who now had stopped in her tracks. "Alright, alright, I'm done. For now."

In the workroom at the back of the funeral home, Chief Goodman straightened up from examining the body of Mr. Morton and surveyed the work space of the man now lying dead. Many pine boxes, mostly adult-sized but some child-sized as well, lined the western wall. The north wall was home to three metal racks of oak caskets each three levels high and each level wide enough for two caskets to reside side by side. In the north eastern corner, squatted a pot-bellied stove with a neighboring box of kindling and a woven basket full of bits of used fabric and old newspapers. Not far from the stove, a door on the eastern wall led outside. The chief knew there was a woodpile outside the door. Beside the door was the only window in the room under which stood a worktable about six feet long. Cupboards under the table itself contained woodworking tools, paintbrushes and cans of wood stains. A sewing machine and fabric cutting table framed the southeastern corner. The southern wall held the door which opened into the wide hall that led to the embalming room and the funeral home itself.

The death vignette was laid out in the middle of the room. An oak casket was cradled atop a stretcher-like frame which lifted the casket off the floor about three feet. Inside the casket, lying face down was Mr. Morton. When discovered, the casket lid was closed and another casket was leaning from behind against the lid. Chief Goodman's constable, Joe North, brother of Elva North who worked at the telephone exchange office, had photographed that scene when they'd all been first called in.

"Joe, be sure to take a clear picture of that cut on his head," instructed Chief Goodman. "Let's turn him over so's you can get the best angle. He's going to have to come out anyway. Junior leave the fingerprinting and come give us a hand."

Chief Goodman's son, Nelson Jr., had plans to follow in his father's footsteps and as such was assisting in the investigation. In far less morbid circumstances he'd shown himself adept at documenting fingerprints. Really more for the thrill of playing detective than for any actuality that the police of Willowsdown would use them.

"Hey now, what's this?" asked the chief as the body was lifted and turned over. Mr. Morton's body had hidden a pair of scissors. "Right. I want these fingerprinted as well, Junior."

Chief Goodman studied the dead man. Above his right temple was a place where the skin had been broken but no blood. His eyes were wide open in death as though in surprise. His right arm was bent over his chest and the fist closed. *To hold the scissors?* the chief asked himself.

"Doesn't look like the murderer used the scissors on him," commented Joe. "No blood anywhere."

"If Mr. Morton's prints are the only ones on the scissors then maybe the murderer didn't bring them," offered Nelson Jr.

"Maybe," mused the chief, "or it could mean he wore gloves."

"Or she," put in Joe as he focused his camera.

"Or she," nodded the chief. "When you're done there, Joe, do your developing magic and leave the photos on my desk at the station. Junior and I'll head upstairs to the apartment."

"Right, Chief."

The workroom door opened. All three turned to see Mr. Morton's apprentice, Arthur Poole, standing tentatively in the doorway.

"Arthur, good to see you," Chief Goodman said warmly. "You're just the man I need."

Arthur's gaze was riveted on the face of his former employer. He swallowed and smiled weakly.

"Glad to hear it."

"Have you heard from Dr. Payne?" Chief Goodman nodded at Joe as Joe headed out to the police station's dark room.

Arthur pulled himself up to his full medium height. "No, he's still very ill."

The town's doctor was bedridden with some kind of stomach ailment, meaning that the autopsy on Mr.

Morton's body would have to be delayed until he recovered. In the meantime, the body would have to be put on ice. *Small mercies*, thought the chief. *At least it's winter.*

"Well then, we'll have to go with the ice option."

"If you're ready to have Mr. Morton moved, I've arranged a place for him," said Arthur, stepping further into the room.

"He can be moved. The two of you worked here a lot?" asked Chief Goodman.

"Mr. Morton did. I only helped move around the caskets when needed. Otherwise the room was locked and he kept the key."

"Excuse me, Arthur. Junior, you head on up to the apartment. I'll be right there."

"Sure thing, Da ... Chief," replied Nelson Jr., gathering up the fingerprinting paraphernalia.

"How did you get in here this morning?" asked Chief Goodman, returning his attention to Arthur.

"I walked in. The door was ajar. When I couldn't find him in his office, I just started looking everywhere. I knew he was here because his coat and boots were in the front hall where he keeps them when he's working."

"Do you always expect him to be in his office first thing in the morning?"

"Always. The day began with him giving orders."

The chief looked up from his note jotting. Arthur's face had a closed, hard look to it.

"That never varied?"

"Never."

"Well then, I'll let you attend to Mr. Morton. Leave everything else as it is."

"Yes, sir."

Walking to the door, Chief Goodman stopped and turned around. "By the way; when the body is eventually released, have you been apprenticing long enough to know how to prepare it for burial?"

Arthur looked at the floor and then at the chief.

"Not exactly—but I'll do my best by him."

Later, at the police station, Chief Goodman slumped in his chair and held his head in his hands. What was going on here? A theft and now a murder? His forays into the criminal world had mostly been lost kittens, shop lifting and the like. He'd never dealt with crime at this level. He had to admit—he really wasn't sure how to proceed. He straightened himself in his chair and pulled it closer to the desk, staring blankly at a box filled with neatly bundled piles of paper. He and Nelson Jr. had unearthed Mr. Morton's financial files. The few they'd studied confirmed that he'd been bamboozling people out of money. They now had evidence to charge the fellow but no fellow to charge. Joe was going to comb through the rest of the invoices in case they revealed something that might shed light on his murder. The other box on the chief's desk was a mahogany jewelry case inlaid with strips of ivory. It was a two-layered job just a titch smaller than a breadbox. Lifting the lid on the case, he poked his index finger through the divided segments. It would seem that Mr. Morton applied his ill-gotten gains to jewelry. The box included rings and tie pins and some pretty swell cuff links as well as a horde of women's jewels: brooches, necklaces, bracelets and the like. All pieces were organized according to type: rings with rings, necklaces with necklaces and so on. Each jewelry type was in its own compartment and all compartments were crammed full except the section for brooches. He hardly considered himself to be a man in the know when it came to women's fashions but it seemed to him the pieces looked more like something his mother or grandmother might have worn. He'd have Mrs. Heyer take a look and see if one of them was her brooch. That'd sure be handy. Wrap up the theft neatly without having to charge anyone and just leaving a murder on his hands. So much better, he thought wryly.

"No," said Edith, shaking her head. "Mine is not there."

Dorothea, Edith and Chief Goodman were gazing into Mr. Morton's jewelry case—the shining surface of Dorothea's dining room table an apt setting for its glories.

"To me, all these pieces look impressive," commented Dorothea, waving her hand over the glittering array. "What do you think, Edith?"

"I agree," replied Edith. "In fact, they're quite magnificent."

"You know, Chief, I don't think we ever told you that Edith's brooch is—or was—one of a pair. They were both found and documented in 1923 and then one went missing and Harold, of course, eventually bought the other for Edith. I can't imagine that information would have any bearing on anything we're dealing with now, but I thought you should know." After a moment's pause, she asked, "Do we know if Mr. Morton ever had a wife?"

"I've never heard so. But truth be told, I know very little about him. He kept very much to himself."

Dorothea nodded. "True. He has—well, had—lived here for about eight years and I never got to know him. I had noticed though," she continued, indicating the box, "that he was fond of rings and tie pins. Always mightily decked out was our Mr. Morton. If there was never a Mrs. Morton, then these could have belonged to his mother."

"Who would have been, Mrs. Morton," grinned Edith.

"Yes, thank you, dear sister; you know what I mean," said Dorothea with a droll glare at Edith. Inspecting the box again, she said, "His pieces are in a jumble, but his mother's—or wife's—are neatly arranged."

"Not as fond of brooches apparently," said Edith, indicating the gaps in the brooch compartment of the box.

"I noticed that too," agreed Dorothea. "All the others are completely full."

"Just wondering, Mrs. Montgomery," interrupted the chief, "did you happen to see Mabel Merriweather the other evening? You know, the Guides and Scouts evening? Nelson Jr. saw her walking in the direction of the funeral home."

Dorothea sat expressionless but she felt sick.

"I have to ask," he muttered apologetically.

"I know, Chief." She absentmindedly brushed away non-existent lint from the table.

"I did see her."

"Walking towards the funeral home?"

"Yes. But she could have been heading to the school—maybe there was a meeting of some sort."

"There wasn't. I asked Junior. He told me that when he and Chamberlain walked past the school it was dark."

"Oh."

"According to local gossip, Mr. Morton was paying court to Myrtle which angered Mabel. Can you comment on that?"

"On the courtship of Myrtle or Mabel being angry?"

"Both."

"I know he was courting Myrtle, but I haven't heard directly from Mabel that this upset her," she replied evasively.

"I see. Well, thank you for your time, ladies." He closed the box picked it up and tucked it under his arm.

Taking note of his slumped shoulders, Dorothea said gently, "Let Mrs. White give you a cup of tea on your way out."

Chief Goodman hesitated and then said, "I think I'll do that. Thanks, ma'am."

Chapter 12: Gathering Suspects

Chief Goodman felt like this day would never end. At Mrs. Montgomery's, Mrs. White had served up a piping hot cup of tea along with a slice of mincemeat pie and an earful of gossip. She had a list of people who she was sure would have been glad to bump off that horrible man. Hadn't Dilman's own brother been cheated out of a satin-lined casket for his wife? Not, of course, that his brother would ever consider murder. But there were others who just might have had enough. There was the Austen family. Only two weeks ago, their little one had succumbed to pneumonia. Maybe Mr. Morton had buried their precious child in a cheap casket and then charged them for an expensive one. If he had done such a thing then he deserved what he got. Not, of course, that it was right for people to take matters into their own hands. But grief does strange things to people. And anyway where did this man come from? He just showed up a few years back seemingly with no family and no history. And so on and so on. That was what, not even an hour ago? His brain felt like mush.

The phone at the front desk began ringing. It rang several times before he remembered that his constable, Joe North, wasn't there to answer it. He rolled back his chair and lumbered through his office door to the desk.

"Police station," he barked.

"Chief Goodman, it's Dorothea Montgomery. You've likely already thought of this but in case you haven't, ask Clarence Clarendon to have a look at Mr. Morton's bank account."

"Right. Thanks, Mrs. Montgomery."

"That's all."

"I got them, Dad, Chief," called Nelson Jr. who had bounded in the station door.

"Got what?" he asked replacing the receiver.

"The fingerprints! Oh, and here's a telegram too. From the Toronto constabulary about those cousins of Olive Roberston."

"Oh, right." He glanced over the telegram and then set it on his desk.

"I'll just get the file so we can match 'em."

In spite of his weariness, Chief Goodman smiled to himself. He remembered very clearly the impromptu "fingerprinting party" at the Merriweather farm this past summer. A burbling stream ran through the property, and along its banks a grove of willow trees trailed their leafy tresses. It was the perfect spot for a picnic. Everyone had finished licking their fingers from the ham sandwiches and deviled eggs and pickles. The "everyone" included the Montgomerys and their daughter's children, Edwina and Edwin Quayle, the Johnsons, the Pequegnants, Dr. and Mrs. Payne, Clarence and Fiona Clarendon, his own family and, of course, the Merriweather sisters. Nelson Jr. had recently announced his determination to go into police work and was eager to make headway on his career. As such, he had brought along the fingerprinting kit to practice taking fingerprints. The four Montgomery grandchildren were thrilled to see how it worked and all the others good naturedly offered their fingers for pressing. Under that golden sunshine dappled by the willow leaves, even the slatted wood of his neighbors' folding chairs glowed warmly and they all prattled amiably if somewhat drowsily. The fingerprints were lightheartedly put "on file". But now with a heavy heart he was actually going to put them to use.

"So in the workroom were a whole lot of these prints," said Nelson Jr., pointing to a particular set from the fingerprinting kit. "Mr. Morton's. I can say that because the other prints were for certain Arthur Poole's. These are his," he said, indicating set number two, "and it would make sense that the prints found all over the room would be Mr. Morton's."

"Good thinking."

"Then there was this set, separate from Morton and Poole, on the outside of the door handle. I'll just take a look here," he said, pausing to study the fingerprint files.

"Looks like you've got a fourth set here," observed the chief while Nelson was busy with his scrutiny.

"Yeah. They're from the apartment." More scrutiny and an intake of breath. "Dad, Chief, look at this."

Nelson Jr. pointed to a set of prints from the file. Upon comparing the door handle prints to the prints on file, the chief too took a stricken breath.

"You just caught me; Mrs. Clarendon and I have an evening engagement. I was getting ready to head out," said Clarence Clarendon as he motioned for Chief Goodman to take a seat. Mr. Clarendon's office consisted of mostly glass. As bank manager, his office was on the second floor and windows on three sides allowed him to look out over the bank or out onto the street or into the office next to him. "What can I do for you?"

"It's about Hugh Morton's murder."

"Ah."

"I need you to look into his bank account."

"Not surprising, I suppose."

"I also need you to check into the Merriweather sisters' account."

"The Merriweathers."

"Yes. Let me know if you find any match ups."

"Will do. I have to say though I think it highly unlikely."

"Yes, well, a week ago this whole thing would have seemed 'highly unlikely'."

"Indeed. I'll look into it myself. Will tomorrow morning be soon enough?"

"If it can be early morning."

"It will."

"Right. I'll be off then. Thanks for your time."

"My pleasure."

Both men stood and shook hands. Departing the office, Chief Goodman opened the door in the wall of windows that looked over the bank, and caught sight of Arthur Poole entering the bank with what could only be described as a beaming smile.

He had to confront Mabel Merriweather with the fact that her fingerprints had been found on the doorknob of Mr. Morton's workroom. He hated to do it but it had to be done. No matter what she said about it all, that was it for the day. He didn't want to think for one more minute about this beastly business. He would sleep on it and take a fresh look in the morning. He nosed his car down the Merriweather farm lane. He noted two bundled figures entering the barn. *Those sisters are hard workers*, he thought. In fact, with just the two of them, it beat him when they slept. He slowed down to let Molly the dog feel that she was winning the race between car and canine but kept his eye fixed on her. Molly lived life on the edge and would often suddenly dart across in front of the vehicle with which she was racing. He supposed her intention was to throw her opponent off balance.

"Hello, girl," he said to Molly as he stepped out of the car. "Good run."

Peering into the barn he could see nothing. The final rays of a winter's day made the transition to looking into the barn an exercise in futility; all was dark. He could just make out some movement.

"Hello!" he called

"Hello," replied a man's voice. "Oh, hey, Chief. What brings you here?"

"I could say the same thing."

"We work here," said another man.

"Work here? Since when?"

"Yesterday."

His eyes having adjusted to the dark, Chief Goodman recognized two brothers from a neighboring farm. They were members of a large family so were always looking to make extra money.

"Did you come looking for work?"

"No," said first brother, "the sisters called us and offered us work."

"Wanted us to come everyday for a few hours and muck out stalls or whatever needed doing," continued the second brother.

"I see. The ladies are inside?"

"No. Been gone all day."

"They said something about being able to live a little now."

"I see. Will you be seeing them later?"

"No, they said they'd be home late."

"That's why we're doing the milking."

"I see." He removed his knitted hat and scratched his bald head. "Well, they've left things in good hands. Good day to you."

He hadn't wanted to talk with Mabel but the fact that she wasn't even here somehow seemed sinister. He'd stop by the Imperial on the way home for a pint. Right there was as good a tonic as any for what ailed a man and he was ailing.

"Chief." True to his word, Clarence Clarendon stopped by the police station with his report first thing the following morning.

"Thank you, sir," said Chief Goodman reaching for the papers held out by the bank manager.

"You were right. There were regular payments being deposited by Morton but no corresponding withdrawals from the Merriweather account."

"Oh good!"

"Chief! Chief!" called Joe North, slamming the door of the station. "Sorry, Mr. Clarendon. Wasn't expecting anyone this early."

"Just leaving. Good day to both of you." He tipped his hat and left, quietly closing the door behind him.

"Chief! I found something in Morton's papers. It has to be important!"

"Alright; catch your breath. You didn't happen to stop by the bakery, did you?"

"Didn't think of it. Look at these. Copies of receipts for cash payments every two weeks. Cash paid to Morton. It goes back almost six years."

Chief Goodman examined the receipts.

"These are receipts for payments made to him personally," said Joe, "not to the funeral home. All the other receipts state 'Morton Funeral Services' on them. They're for business. These are different."

Chief Goodman could see they were different. He could also see that the amount of each copied receipt tallied with the regular deposits detailed on the bank account statement left by Mr. Clarendon. But the payments to Mr. Morton had not been coming from the Merriweather sisters. Chief Goodman was sure that Mr. Morton had given a receipt for these payments not for the comfort of the payee, but for his own obviously meticulous record keeping. He would need to speak with Arthur Poole and Dorothea Montgomery.

Dorothea couldn't recall a time when she didn't relish the company of books. The prosaic flatness of them opened into far-off adventures or dreamy romance or intellectual understanding. "There is no frigate like a book to take us lands away, nor any coursers like a page of prancing poetry. This traverse may the poorest take without oppress of toll; how frugal is the chariot that bears a human soul!" Emily Dickinson's poem always came to mind when she picked up a book.

Her mother, Magdalena Springfield, had been such a "bluestocking" that her parents had, according to her mother, "literally wrung their hands" with anxiety that she would never find a man who would be interested in her or (more relevantly from her mother's point of view) be interesting. Magdalena grew up in Oxford and through her brothers had access to the Bodleian Library. Her hunger for learning and reasoned thinking was something she cultivated in her children, finding receptive ground in each of them with fruitful and varying harvests.

Dorothea wasn't able to cull the depths of Bodleian academia but since its opening in 1914, Willowsdown's library benefited from a forward thinking head librarian who insisted on a wide range of backdated newspapers as well as the newly emerging microfiche technology. So this morning found Dorothea surrounded by the society pages of British, and local newspapers, some from as far back as ten years. She really had no idea what she was looking for: just something that might shed light on Edith's brooch's history or the kind of people who might steal it. Or murder for it? Mr. Morton's murder seemed to her to confirm that this must be "an outside job" as they said in those ridiculous detective movies. It seemed an age since the Livingstones' party and the disappearance of Edith's brooch. The only people from out of town that night were Chester and Eleanor Smith, Olive Robertson's cousins. It was definitely a shot in the dark but she needed to do something. Her reasoning was that apart from the obvious strategy of unearthing articles that outlined finds from archaeological digs of the last number of years, she would look into the society pages. Pages that described the doings of people with more money and time than they knew what to do with just might make some reference to the Smiths.

It was after an hour of slugging through descriptions of Miss So and So wearing organza and lilies-of-the-valley at another Miss So and So's wedding or tea party or picnic or whatever, that she picked up a British paper just for variety. Turning over a few pages, she noticed a half sheet spread with the headline "High Society Heists" and underneath it a square of four pictures each showing a group of about fifteen people and dated May 1923.

So which one was it? Ten years ago, a group of friends gypsyied about the countryside for four months staying at the stately homes of our nation's best known. After each visit, a piece of jewelry went missing. To date none of the pieces have been recovered. Of the group, only four remained in Great Britain; the others were dead of natural causes, killed in the Great War or emigrated.

The article continued on, but Dorothea had focused in on one of the names under the pictures: Fiona Plowden. The image of Fiona Plowden was unmistakable as the now Mrs. Fiona Clarendon. In slow motion, Dorothea leaned back in her chair and exhaled the breath she hadn't realized she'd been holding. The writer of the article had outlined in detail each of the pieces—description, history, from whom they had been stolen. Of the four items, there was not one necklace, not one pair of earrings, nor a ring of any kind. All the pieces stolen had been brooches.

Back at home, Gladys told her that Chief Goodman had telephoned to say he would be stopping by later and needed to speak with her.

"Thank you, Gladys. By the way, how is your mother faring?"

"My mother? Oh yes, thank you for asking, Mrs. Montgomery; she is holding her own at the moment."

"Glad to hear it. But you still need to leave us after Christmas?"

"Yes, I believe I do."

"Our loss then. Did Chief Goodman mention anything about Mrs. Heyer's brooch?"

"No, ma'am."

"Very well." She nodded and smiled signaling Gladys' dismissal.

It was while the Montgomery household was finishing their dinner that Chief Goodman stopped by. As she welcomed him, Dorothea was asking herself whether or not to share with him what she had discovered about Fiona Clarendon while at the library. Surely that was too long ago to be connected with what was going on in Willowsdown at present. She'd wait and see what the chief had to say.

"Chief Goodman, good of you to come over. Please sit with us for dessert. Will your sister and her family be joining you for Christmas this year?"

He settled into the proffered chair as Dianna and Gladys served plum preserves and pound cake.

"They will. Mary's all in a tizzy because they arrive later this afternoon. With everything that's been going on, I haven't been around to help her as I usually do. The young ones have been picking up the slack though. You'll see my sister tomorrow evening at the Christmas Eve service."

"Do you have any news of Grandmama's brooch, Chief Goodman?" asked Alice.

"Nothing that's worth being rewarded with this dessert. By the way, Mrs. Montgomery, I will need a wee word with you in private."

"I take it then that you aren't going to pull my brooch out of your hat," said Edith.

"You take it right. I contacted the Toronto police force when the Smiths and Violet Hacker headed there after the Livingstone party. Telegram came yesterday saying they made enquiries and searches but found nothing. The Smiths have impeccable reputations. The only slight discoloration of the picture, so to speak," he cleared his throat, "is that Violet was seen in lengthy conversation at some party with a fellow who deals in antique jewelry. But then again, absolutely nothing connects her and the stolen article."

"Nor will there be," said Dorothea stoutly.

"I'm sure you're right," mumbled the chief through his cake.

"So the search stays focused in Willowsdown," observed George.

"I'm afraid so."

"How goes the Morton case?" enquired Charles.

All eyes were on the chief as he choked back his last morsel of dessert.

"Can't really say. I do need to speak with you though, Mrs. Montgomery."

"About the Morton case?" asked Dorothea with surprise.

"'fraid so."

"Well, then. Certainly. Let's go to the library. Please excuse us," she said, rising from the table.

Settled into chairs before a golden fire, Chief Goodman began, "I'm taking you into my confidence, Mrs. Montgomery. Well, into police confidence really."

She nodded encouragingly.

"It's come to my attention that Lillian Poole was paying Mr. Morton regular sums of money over a period of about six years."

"Arthur Poole's mother? Whatever for?"

"Don't know. It wasn't a business transaction."

Dorothea's eyes widened. "Blackmail!"

"Looks like it. You've lost a son. I thought maybe you could talk with her, sort of mother to mother, and find out what this money is all about."

"My son wasn't killed in the war though."

"No, but it's still a gaping loss."

Dorothea lowered her eyes to the hands in her lap. "Very true," she replied quietly. "I will certainly do what I can."

"Much appreciated. I think you'll get more from her than would an official police questioning."

"Chief," she said slowly, "blackmail is a motive for murder."

He met her troubled gaze. "I know."

Chapter 13: It Doesn't Look Good

For the last few years it had become a tradition for Dorothea's friend, Edwina Quayle, and her husband Edwin to share a Christmas brunch at Dorothea's. Typically all the staff were "off duty" as of Christmas Eve until December 27 so the brunch consisted of leftovers from Christmas Day and any new culinary delight Edwina felt like concocting. The resulting smorgasbord was made up of a complete muddle of flavors; but that was half the fun.

George snatched the last pig-in-a-blanket off the plate.

"These are the absolute kipper's knickers, Mrs. Q," he said, scarfing down a wrapped frankfurter.

"Thank you, George. For myself, I prefer Mrs. White's fruit cake," she said, as she in turn reached for her fourth piece.

"Speaking of pigs-in-a-blanket: I ran into George Flesherton on my walk this morning," began Charles, stirring his coffee. "He's the town's butcher," he explained, enlightening Edith, Alice and George. "Poor man. He was sitting on the steps of his shop absolutely blanched in the face. He said he had come to the shop because he'd forgotten to take bacon home before Christmas. He'd also forgotten that Mr. Morton's body was in his cooler and when he walked in this morning he almost had a heart attack."

"Help is on the way," said Edwin Quayle. "Apparently Dr. Payne is on the mend."

"When do you think he'll get to the autopsy?" asked Alice.

"If not tomorrow certainly the next day," said Charles.

"That'll give Chief Goodman something more to go on," commented George.

"He certainly doesn't have much, does he?" remarked Edith. "You're very quiet, Dorothea."

"Oh, just imagining the fright George Flesherton must have had—not the most pleasant way to begin a day."

"Have you heard from Gladys as to her mother's welfare?" asked Alice.

Gladys' plan had been to stay until after Christmas at which time she was leaving for good to care for her ailing mother. On Christmas Eve day, she informed Dorothea that her mother had taken a turn for the worse and her presence at home was urgently required.

"I haven't," said Dorothea, "and I realized I have no way to contact her. She was going to leave her address but I suppose in her rush to catch the train it must have slipped her mind. I hope all is well with her. Mrs. White loaded Gladys up with jars of beef broth which she swears is efficacious in healing all illness. If Gladys has been feeding her mother all that Mrs. White sent, then Mrs. Cooper should be well and truly on the mend," laughed Dorothea.

"As they say, 'no news is good news'," said Charles. "Let's assume that's true in Gladys' case."

"She seemed like a smart girl," offered Edith. "I'm sure if there was anything to tell she'd be quick to let you know."

"I agree," said George. "Too bad Mrs. White didn't leave some of that beef broth for us. It'd be just the thing with this cranberry sauce," said he, spooning the last of it onto his plate.

For the Montgomery household, the rest of the day would be spent in playing various board games and in reminiscences. Before bracing herself for a game of spoons, Dorothea placed a phone call to Mrs. Poole asking that lady if she would be free the following day. Dilman would be dispatched to pick her up and bring her to Dorothea's for a morning visit if that suited her. It did.

For Chief Goodman, the day was not shaping up in an equally agreeable manner. There was a dead body in the butcher's cooler which wasn't unusual except that, unlike that of the animal carcasses, the cause of Mr. Morton's demise was still unknown. The chief's sister and family were staying on into the day and leaving before supper but he and Nelson Jr. bade their adieus and were now huddled with Joe North in the chief's office. They had been examining the photographs of the crime scene.

"Mr. Morton, face down in the casket," murmured the chief. "Lid closed. Another casket leaning on that lid."

"A cut on his head, but no blood," continued Joe, holding up the close-up shot of Mr. Morton's face.

"And no blood anywhere else even though there were scissors under the body," said Nelson Jr. "Jeepers!" he exclaimed, slapping his forehead. "I didn't fingerprint the scissors!"

"Do it now, son," asserted the chief. "And let me see that fourth set of prints. We didn't look into them any further after finding Mabel Merriweather's on the doorknob. These were from Mr. Morton's apartment you said?" he asked, reaching for the police fingerprint files.

"Yes, sir," replied Nelson Jr.

"Sir, do you want me to question Mabel Merriweather?" asked Joe.

Chief Goodman sighed. "Someone'll have to. Can't say I've had any more experience in this than you have so's you might as well. But call ahead before you go."

"Right. Shall I ring her now?"

The chief sighed again. "Might as well."

Joe left the office to call from the phone at the front desk and Chief Goodman returned his attention to the fingerprints. Given the paucity of samples on file, it didn't take long to determine whether or not there was a match.

He lifted his head to find Nelson Jr. looking at him.

"Fiona Clarendon's" he stated. At the same instant, Nelson Jr. blurted, "Arthur Poole's."

"No answer," remarked Joe, retracing the few steps to the office. "What?" he asked glancing from father to son.

"This set of fingerprints, found in Mr. Morton's apartment, are Fiona Clarendon's and Junior says the ones on the scissors are Arthur Poole's."

Joe whistled. "What now?"

"Now," the chief replied, rubbing his bald head, "I think we have to arrest Arthur Poole. It doesn't look good for him. He has a motive for killing Morton—the blackmailing of his mother. We know he was at the scene according to the prints on the scissors."

"And his prints are on the casket that was leaning against the one Mr. Morton was lying in," offered Nelson Jr.

"They likely would be anyway since he helped Morton move caskets," said Joe.

"Yeah, I guess so," nodded Nelson Jr.

"What about Mrs. Clarendon?" asked Joe.

"I have an idea about that," said the chief, "but I want to think about it a bit. There could be a perfectly normal reason that her prints were in his apartment. It'd be different if they'd been found in the workroom. We'll leave her for a moment. Arthur on the other hand…."

"Yeah," Joe and Nelson Jr. agreed heavily.

Chief Goodman sighed—yet again. "Junior, you stay and put things away. Joe, you'd better come along with me." He glanced towards the police station's solitary cell. "We shouldn't be long," he said, pulling on his wool cap.

"No, no, no, no, no! You can't do this!" sobbed Lillian Poole, clutching her son's hand. "Not, Arthur! He didn't do it!"

"I'm very sorry, ma'am, but as I said we do have evidence to suggest otherwise." Chief Goodman placed his hand on Arthur's shoulder. "Arthur Poole, it is my disagreeable duty to arrest you for the murder of Hugh Morton. I wish to give you the following warning: you need not say anything. You have nothing to hope from any promise or favor and nothing to fear from any threat whether or not you say anything. Anything you do or say may be used as evidence. Do you understand?"

Arthur Poole nodded. "Yes, sir. Ma, you need to let me go."

"Mrs. Poole, if you'll just sit over here," said Joe, gently leading her to a kitchen chair. "Would you like me to bring over one of your other sons?"

Mrs. Poole quit crying abruptly. She twitched a handkerchief out of her cardigan sleeve. From her seat, she looked up fiercely and said, "No, but you can take me right over to Dorothea Montgomery's!"

Lillian Poole was an intelligent, hard-working woman who had energetically raised four sons. Her husband had died six years ago and in light of being a hard worker and a steady saver, as well as far-seeing, in that he'd bought a generous life insurance package, he had left her financially comfortable. However, shortly after his death, she chose to take a full-time position as a bank teller. Her oldest son never returned from the Great War. Her two middle sons were both married and lived in town and, Arthur, her youngest, had been apprenticed to Hugh Morton. Now she was in the unenviable position of a mother whose son has been accused of murder. Mrs. Montgomery had requested her presence tomorrow morning but tomorrow morning was not soon enough. She had heard that Mrs. Montgomery possessed an astute mind as well as a gracious understanding of human frailty. She would tell her everything.

"Charles," began Dorothea. They were settled in armchairs in the sitting area of their bedroom. After several rowdy rounds of spoons, Edwina and Edwin had returned home, and Alice and George were leaning over a chess board with furrowed brows. Edith had helped herself to Dorothea's Dorothy Sayers' novel and was duly absorbed. Dorothea and Charles were taking some time to themselves before everyone regrouped around a game of Chinese checkers.

"Mmmm?"

"Edwina tells me that the Merriweather sisters are going ahead with insurance."

"Pardon? The Merriweather sisters? Yes."

"Did you offer them special terms?"

"Special terms? No."

"I wonder what made them change their minds."

No answer.

"I hope it's everything they imagine it to be."

Charles turned over a newspaper sheet.

"What I imagine it to be for them is peace of mind, which is worth a lot."

"Yes, worth a lot."

Silence.

"It's a rather sudden turn of events, wouldn't you say?"

"Well, you know them; once they make up their minds...."

"They came to the office on Christmas Eve day, is that right?"

"That's right."

Another silence.

"I suppose they only bought the most basic package."

Charles peered over his paper.

"Dorothea." He dropped the paper into his lap. "What is all this about?"

She tilted her head and bit her lip.

"You're suspecting them of something?" he asked incredulous.

"Well!" she exclaimed sheepish and defiant at the same time. "Where is this money coming from to get insurance all of a sudden?"

Charles gazed at her in troubled silence.

"You know," he said. "At noon that day Clarence Clarendon was coming into the Imperial for dinner at the same time I was and he remarked about me likely seeing the Merriweather sisters soon—something about an unexpected windfall. They had been to the bank that morning."

"Depositing money?"

"He didn't specify, of course; it was just a passing comment while exchanging pleasantries. You aren't seriously thinking that Mabel Merriweather murdered Hugh Morton?"

"Noooo. But what if they stole Edith's brooch and cashed it in?"

"Well, they could hardly do that with Clarendon. He knows there's a stolen brooch out there."

"Maybe they didn't deal with Mr. Clarendon."

"You mean someone else at the bank? The assistant manager?"

"No, someone who might know about gems and have access to ready cash."

"Such as?"

"Fiona Clarendon."

"Fiona Clarendon?" He stared at her blankly. "Why on earth Fiona Clarendon?"

"Because Fiona Clarendon is no stranger to precious jewelry. Just a minute." In the bookcase behind her, pressed between two books, was the library article about the jewel thefts from various English country homes. She withdrew it and handed it to Charles. "Read this."

Charles read.

"You need to bring that article to Nelson's attention," he stated when finished.

"Dorothea? Are you up there?" called Edith. "You have a visitor. I believe her name is Lillian Poole."

An hour and a half later, Dorothea was in her room again fingering the "High Society Heists" article about the theft of expensive brooches from English country homes in 1913. When Joe North left Mrs. Poole with Dorothea, he advised her that he and the chief would be at the station all day. And that was where she needed to be. There was much to share. To keep the newspaper clipping safe, she slipped it into the pages of a book but as she was closing the book her eye caught a name in the article. Bertram Somerville. Bertram Somerville. Where had she heard that name? She plucked the paper from the pages of the book and perused the article. This Mr. Somerville was one of the group of friends who had "gypsied about the countryside" along with Fiona Clarendon. In fact, in three of the four pictures, according to the captions, he was standing next to her. She stood grasping the paper, staring at her bedroom wall as though the files in her brain were on a visible screen that could be examined. And there it was. She remembered now where she had heard that name. She restored the article to its place inside the book and stuffed the book into her favorite wooden handled chintz bag.

"Dorothea!" called Charles. "I've taken Mrs. Poole home. Do you want the car or are you walking?"

"Oh, walking. I have things to turn over in my mind."

On descending the stairs to the front hall, she found Charles holding her coat and a sober family group each offering a piece of winter wear.

The police station neighbored the post office, each looking in different directions on a pie-shaped corner in the town's square if one could call it that with such an odd angle in its midst. Dorothea stamped the snow off her boots outside the door and stepped into the perfectly square room with the black and white checkerboard floor. To the left was a tall counter behind which Joe North was perched on a stool, behind him a hedge of filing cabinets. On the wall above the cabinets was a framed picture of King George V and a calendar from the town's creamery displaying the twelfth and final cow for the year—some kind of a bovine pin-up Dorothea had always presumed. To the right was a lone, and almost always empty, cell lined with the cast off pages of said creamery's past calendars. Evidently Chief Goodman imagined all those cowy eyes might seem so gently rebuking that any inhabitant of the cell would break down and confess all. That cell, of course, was not empty now and Dorothea fervently hoped that Arthur Poole had nothing to confess.

"Afternoon, Mrs. Montgomery," said Joe solemnly. "We thought you might be coming around."

"Good afternoon, Joe. I need to speak with Chief Goodman," she quietly said, glancing towards the chief's empty office.

She took the few steps that would bring her in front of the cell. "Hello, Arthur. I'm sorry to see you here. I've been talking with your mother and she's told me everything. What do you have to say about the evening of Mr. Morton's death?"

"I was at home all evening. I was studying."

Dorothea nodded. "Thank you, Arthur. Your mother has asked me to share what she told me with Chief Goodman."

Arthur groaned. "That will make things look very bad, but I didn't do it!"

She studied him intently. "If you didn't kill Hugh Morton then the truth will out. Chief Goodman will not stop until he's certain as to what happened."

She turned back to the front desk and Joe North.

"The chief stepped out to stretch his legs," said Joe, explaining the chief's absence. "Grandpa decided to open the bakery today so I wouldn't be surprised if he came back with half a dozen of Grandpa's doughnuts. That's usually what happens when he stretches his legs; he just happens to stroll past the bakery."

They both smiled. It felt good to speak of lighthearted things.

"I can wait."

The station door opened revealing a frosty Chief Goodman with a paper bag tucked under his arm. "Get the coffee on, Joe. Your Grandpa saw me passing and insisted I take some doughnuts."

Joe grinned at Dorothea on his way to the tiny pot-bellied stove where a kettle of water stayed warm for any refreshment needs.

"Mrs. Montgomery. I hoped you'd be around. I'll just get plates for Joe and Arthur's share of the doughnuts. Have a seat here and I'll be right in." He pulled a battered armchair, likely a cast off from the Goodman home, from a corner of his office and offered her a seat. "What will you be having in your coffee?"

"Just cream, please."

"Coffee for you, Arthur?" he asked kindly.

"Uh, oh, yes, please."

"Got some doughnuts here too if you'd like," offered Joe.

"Thanks."

After serving Arthur his coffee and doughnut and relocking the cell, Joe quietly closed the office door so the chief and Mrs. Montgomery could talk privately and took his coffee and doughnut behind the front desk where he could keep his eye on his less than rowdy prisoner.

"Now then," began Chief Goodman after the mugs of coffee and plate of doughnuts were in front of them and he was settled in his swivel chair, "what can you tell me?"

Chief Goodman remembered the day twelve years ago when he was in Joe North's position and the former chief had been sitting just where he was now and Mrs. Montgomery had been sitting just where she was. But that day she went toe to toe with his boss, elucidating her points regarding her opinion that her son, Leland's, death was accidental whereas his boss was determined on the more dramatic charge, against a neighborhood boy, of murder. At the time, as a sergeant, he'd been impressed by her grasp of the situation and entirely convinced of the rightness of her conclusions. Thankfully, Mrs. Montgomery was proven right and ever since then he'd had a profound respect for her perceptive abilities.

Dorothea drew in a breath and lay her chintz bag on the desk.

"I'll begin with Mrs. Poole but in here," she indicated her bag, "I have other information that may have a crucial bearing on the theft of Edith's brooch, which, I suppose, we may find to be linked with Mr. Morton's murder ... though I can't see why." She took a bite of a doughnut, chewed and swallowed.

"Just thinking how best to keep a long story short," she began. "Hugh Morton was blackmailing Lillian Poole because her oldest son, Adam, was an army deserter not a casualty of war."

"What?" Chief Goodman, who had been taking a slurp of coffee spurted it over the desk. "Sorry," he mumbled, patting the desk top with his pocket handkerchief.

"It seems that Adam deserted his post in 1916. The Pooles were informed but were so heartsick and ashamed they let on that he had been killed. Apparently Adam wrote to them after the Armistice explaining why he left the army. As you may remember, he was a soft-spoken, gentle fellow, very much like Arthur. He told them it was horrible beyond imagining and he reached a point where he couldn't stand it anymore. He asked if he could come home. Mr. Poole wrote back saying that he was dead to them."

Dorothea was silent and then took a sip of coffee.

"Without going into detail, Hugh Morton met Adam Poole in Europe and somehow or other learned that he had deserted. When Mr. Morton moved to Willowsdown—lo and behold—he heard of a family by the name of Poole whose son, Adam, was killed in action: except that he knew differently. It wasn't until Mr. Poole died in 1920 that Morton started extorting money from Lillian—too much of a coward to extort money from a man. Last year, inadvertently through, I think, a teacher at the high school, Mr. Morton heard that Arthur was interested in going into the funeral business. He offered to apprentice Arthur but at no pay, all a part of the extortion he was extracting, and blessed little training, according to Mrs. Poole."

Dorothea sat silent again before beginning quietly but firmly, "I know of very few veterans who want to talk of the war. They may tell inconsequential stories but they share nothing of significance. It seems to me they've been scarred in ways we can't understand. And the few who are beginning to talk are quickly criticized and muffled because what they reveal is not the stuff of glory. I can't quite say where I stand on all this as I do love the Empire but I also know the searing pain of losing a child. Mrs. Poole has lost Adam twice. It will take a confession from Arthur or incontrovertible evidence for me to believe that he killed Mr. Morton. I will do everything in my power to work to prove him innocent so that this mother does not lose another son."

Chief Goodman cleared his throat. "Your information doesn't make things look good for Arthur," he said in a low voice. "And according to his statement, he was home studying last night with his mother as the only witness to his alibi. I'm not saying Lillian Poole would lie or that mothers in general will lie for their children but," he cleared his throat again, "we all know how fierce is a mother's love. I'm not sure you're seeing this objectively."

She looked at him levelly. "I'm not, but I can still think clearly."

"I will proceed according to the law if everything points against him."

"I know—as you should. We just need to find who really did it."

Chief Goodman sighed and rubbed his head, "Yes and there's the rub."

"Let's put the murder aside for a moment. I want you to read the article I have here." She pulled the book from her bag and smoothed the newspaper article out in front of him. "I'll warm up my coffee while you read. Would you like some more?" she asked as she stood to exit the office and pluck the coffee pot from the potbellied stove.

"No, thanks," he replied, already reading.

"There's not much left," said Joe ruefully as she poured out the coffee.

"Just enough and it's still nice and hot," she said, cupping the mug in her hands. "I hear Chamberlain Johnson has already gone back to school. I thought he was home for a bit yet. Didn't the two of you have plans to finish working on some car?"

"We were going to work on Grandpa's 1912 Model T, but Chamberlain got some telegram this morning and went haring off back to Ridley."

"Must have been important."

Joe shrugged. "I guess so. His mother's plenty mad though at him flying off like that."

"Yes, it would be disappointing for them. They were so looking forward to him being home for the holiday."

Chief Goodman cleared his throat. Dorothea saluted Joe with her mug and stepped back into the office.

"This could put a whole different spin on everything," said the chief, tapping the article. "Fiona Clarendon mixed up in jewelry thefts?"

"You said that Fiona Clarendon's fingerprints were in Mr. Morton's apartment. There must have been some connection between them."

"Her fingerprints weren't in the workroom though where he was found."

"No. Hmmm."

"I hate to bring this up but the fact is that Mabel Merriweather's were found on the doorknob."

"No!"

"Yes. Nowhere else as far as we could find."

Dorothea sat thoughtfully then said, "Just before coming here, Charles confirmed that the sisters have bought life insurance—something they hadn't done because of the payments. Now it seems they have the money for it. It occurred to me that perhaps, I despise saying this, they stole the brooch and then Mrs. Clarendon gave them cash for it."

"But how would they ever know of her past?"

"That's definitely the weak point in my theory. But here's another possible trail to follow. This fellow here," she pointed to a man in the article photo named Bertram Somerville. "This is the man who sold Edith's brooch to her husband."

Chapter 14: Wonderings

After returning home from the police station, Dorothea sat herself down at her writing desk. Gladys' sudden departure meant that she was in need of another staff member which gave her an excuse to call on Fiona Clarendon. Fiona Clarendon always seemed to know where to find new staff. This was a good thing as Dorothea's house help tended not to stay in her employ for long. Either she was not a good judge of character or she was difficult to work for. Certainly it was true that there were fewer and fewer women entering domestic service and Dorothea had to admit she couldn't blame them so it was getting more troublesome to secure house help.

She felt badly for Gladys. Although domestic service wasn't glamorous it did allow a young woman, depending on her situation, to see more of the world and get out of her parents' home. She had been surprised at Gladys' choice of work though. Gladys seemed to be actually quite well educated. If her mother never recovered, or never recovered fully, Gladys could have her life stunted by being trapped at home raising younger siblings and overseeing a household not her own. Settling the notepaper in front of her, she dipped her pen and wrote:

Mrs. Clarendon,
I wondered if I might call on you tomorrow morning at 9:30. I have a domestic matter on which I would so appreciate your input.

Dorothea Montgomery

Tucking the note into an envelope, she headed to the
kitchen to find Dilman and dispatch him to the
Clarendons. She entered to hear Dianna saying to Mrs.
White, "My sister said, that Amelia Fletcher told her
that Chamberlain said that Mrs. Johnson is cross at him.
Chamberlain hadn't told his parents that he was leaving
so soon. Mrs. Johnson said she doesn't understand why
he didn't rest a while longer at home since he's worked
so hard at school. Plus it was so secretive she said.
She's afraid there's some danger or some such thing!
But my sister said that Amelia said that he went back
early to work out something about money—supposedly
lots of it."

Mrs. White was peeling potatoes for the evening
meal and Dianna was taking a break from her tasks.

"Amelia and your sister are good friends, aren't
they?" asked Dorothea.

"Yes, Mrs. Montgomery, best friends—they tell
each other everything. Amelia wasn't quite happy with
him either while he was home because he seemed so
distracted. She hoped maybe he would give her a
promise ring. She even saw him at Pequegnants'
jewelry store after the Livingstone party and thought for
sure he was looking at something for her but she never
got anything."

"I thought his parents had plans for him to go to
school in the old country," commented Mrs. White.

"They do."

"He's still wanting to go, isn't he?" asked Dorothea.

"I think so. I think that's why he's excited about this
money thing; it will help to get him there sooner," said
Dianna.

"To be sure then it would be best for Miss Amelia Fletcher's heart to not be pining after doodads or young Chamberlain. Looking for a career herself is what she should be about, to my way of thinking," announced Mrs. White.

There was a snort at the end of the long kitchen table from Dilman who was reading the newspaper.

"If she's going to look for work, she'd best stay close by. Once you go out into those big cities there's no end of people involved in funny business. Right here's an article about some couple owning a respectable jewelry business who've been accused of making paste jewelry and selling it as the real thing. And then another article about some phone exchange office where the owner and all the operators were in on blackmail schemes. That Violet had best watch out now that she's let herself be whisked off to Toronto." He shook his head as if to say he washed his hands of any repercussions accrued by Violet from big city associations.

"You're talking like a daft person," said Mrs. White. "Violet's a good girl. Isn't she staying here now after Christmas to help her mother?"

He shook his head again but said nothing.

"Anyway, I don't think Amelia would want to move that far from home," said Dianna.

"Well, then. She'd best put Master Johnson out of her head being that Oxford is a sight further than where Violet's going," remarked Mrs. White sagely. "And now that the potatoes done, is there something I can be getting for you, Mrs. Montgomery?"

"I'm needing the services of your husband, Mrs. White. Dilman, sorry to disturb your reading but this note must be taken to Mrs. Clarendon post haste."

There was nothing more she could do today to uncover beetle brooches or a Morton murderer. Alice and George had invited the readers' club over for the evening and she was content to stir up some hot cocoa for them; she had already taken them some shortbread. They were gathered in the morning room, so from the kitchen she could just catch the drift of their conversation. None of them had made much headway with *The Great Gatsby*, the book of their choice, but jaunty discussion was ensuing.

"I disagree. Nick Caraway describes himself as non-judgmental and yet it seems he views himself as morally above the others," asserted Violet Hacker.

"Maybe he is," countered Elva North. "So far the other characters aren't admirable."

"What makes someone admirable?" posited Olive Robertson

"Honesty," said Elva.

"Fair play," said Nelson Jr. Goodman.

"Humility," said Alice.

"Kindness," offered George.

"Selflessness," put in Isaac Kingswood.

"Doesn't sound like anyone in our book so far," remarked Alice.

"I can't see how slithering from primordial ooze, as some scientists would have it, would give us a compass to uphold such qualities and conversely be outraged at violence and injustice, etc.," remarked Elva.

"One can't last long without honesty and fair play and so on," said George.

"True. But it still doesn't answer why we think highly of them. If we are only creatures of instinct and survival of the fittest is our only modus operandi then we would applaud a dog eat dog mentality rather than those qualities we just listed," replied Elva.

"I can hardly believe what's happened in sleepy old Willowsdown! A murder! And here I thought going to the big city was where I'd need to be careful," exclaimed Violet.

"And a theft," interposed Isaac.

"Oh, right, of course," murmured Violet.

"Human beings wouldn't last long if we thought thievery and murder and so on was all right," said Nelson Jr.

"I suppose even the ancients, before the Ten Commandments and all that, looked for moral direction to what they considered higher rather than looking to something lower," commented Nelson Jr.

"For the ancients, Ewan MacMurray is your man. By the way, did you see him while you were in town?" George asked Violet.

"Yes, I did see him once and met the friends he's staying with as well—very sophisticated and pleasant people. They own a number of jewelry stores in the city but I think they have some connection with archaeology. Well, maybe not connection but an interest anyhow. I suppose that's what linked them with Ewan and his father."

"And you'll soon be returning to Toronto," commented Alice, casting a glance at George who was handing the plate of shortbread to Elva.

"Oh yes! I'll be working at Simpson's. Lots of opportunity for advancement; maybe even buying trips to New York."

"Your mother has trained you well," said Olive.

"She has. I've much to be thankful for. I've enjoyed myself thoroughly these last several weeks but being apart from her does have an ache."

"Your kindness in putting off starting your job to help her train a new girl will go a long way in making things easier for her," encouraged Elva.

"I wonder if the two are connected," mused George, apparently oblivious to the aforesaid conversation.

"The two what?" asked Violet.

"Well, the theft and the murder," rejoined George.

"Impossible," Violet declared.

"What say you?" asked George of Nelson Jr. "You're on the case."

"I'm not saying anything. Sorry to sound stuffy but it's police business," said Nelson Jr.

"Of course, of course. Sorry old man. Didn't mean to put you on the spot," said George.

"We'd better get back to our book discussion," remarked Elva. "We're wandering into forbidden territory."

"Right ho. Now what were you saying about Nick Caraway, Violet?" asked George eagerly.

Chapter 15: Which One is doing the Outwitting?

"Mrs. Montgomery, how good to see you," Fiona Clarendon said smoothly as, the following morning, she ushered Dorothea into the Clarendon hallway. "I see you walked," she commented, *rather caustically*, Dorothea thought. "Well, it's good for the heart they say. How are your sister and her grandchildren enjoying their stay?"

Dorothea sat down in the proffered chair.

"Oh, I'm sorry," Mrs. Clarendon continued, "that's a thoughtless question. I suppose for the most part it's been upsetting."

"It has cast its shadow. But Edith is philosophical about the brooch. She recognizes that ultimately it's only a thing. It hurts more because her husband had taken such pains to acquire it for her. Of course, in relation to the murder, it pales in significance. She never knew Mr. Morton but any murder is shocking." Taking a gamble, she continued, "I understand you've known him for many years so I suppose you've lost a friend." Dorothea blinked innocently at Mrs. Clarendon.

"How do you know that?"

"Well, now, let me think; how do I know that? Could it have been the Merriweather sisters who mentioned it?"

"I can't imagine. But, yes, I met him before the war and we renewed our acquaintance when he moved to town. I wouldn't call him a friend but as you say, any murder is shocking."

"I know—knew—very little of Mr. Morton. Was he from where you lived back home?"

"No, we met on the continent."

"I have to admit, Mrs. Clarendon, to my chagrin, I've never taken the time to ask you about your home and family. Is your family still in the old country?"

"I was an only child. Both my parents are dead."

"I'm very sorry. Where did you grow up?"

"I grew up in Yorkshire."

"I was born and lived in England for 15 years, but I never saw the beauty of the Dales—my loss, of course. You went south at some point though?"

"Yes. We settled in Oxford where my father was from originally. As a young man he had moved north for the manufacturing."

"Such a small world! My mother grew up in Oxford so I have roots there too. What brought your father back?"

"His father had been an academic at the university; my father hadn't. They parted ways in an unhappy manner and stayed apart. When my grandfather died I believe my father felt the tug of his roots."

"Was your father able to pick up where he left off with family and friends?"

"For the most part."

"I hope that helped you to make a new circle of friends."

"It did. I suppose I must have felt the ancestral pull as well. My mother was a Yorkshire girl born and bred. She died when I was six. Without her, that's perhaps why I never entirely embraced my northern heritage. Oxford somehow felt familiar from the first so friendships fell easily into place."

"I wonder if we know any of the same people ... let me see .... Well, of course, my uncles stayed there. They were Springfields—David and George."

"I can't say those name are familiar."

"Or any of the Nichols?"

Mrs. Clarendon had picked up a small covered ashtray and was flapping the lid open and shut.

"But then there were also the Somersets—no—Somervilles. My sister kept up with them. I think they had a country house nearby, didn't they?" Dorothea tilted her head ingenuously.

Mrs. Clarendon stopped clicking the lid.

"The Somervilles? No, they didn't have country property. They weren't from Oxford."

"I must be thinking of someone else. But then I was quite positive ..."

"Mrs. Montgomery," broke in Fiona Clarendon, looking at her watch, "I don't want to seem rude but how can I help you address your domestic matter?"

"Oh dear, I'm sorry to be taking up so much of your time. I'll get to the point...."

As it turned out, Mrs. Clarendon did know of a friend of a friend who was moving to a smaller house and was reducing her house help. The requisite information was exchanged and Dorothea left in high hopes of soon filling the gap left by Gladys. About the other matter, she was less sanguine. Fiona Clarendon readily admitted to knowing Hugh Morton so it could be as straightforward as she said: two former acquaintances meeting in the same town years later. She also admitted to knowing somebody by the name of Somerville and knowing them well enough to be sure of facts involving real estate and geography. But then that was the kind of general knowledge anyone might have. Dorothea really was no further ahead. Her only consolation was that Fiona had not eagerly played the do-we-know-the-same-people game which might suggest she wanted to avoid further disclosures. And she had either been truly pressed for time or had neatly directed the conversation, leaving Dorothea with the question of who was leading whom?

On her walk home, Chief Goodman pulled up beside her.

"Morning, Mrs. Montgomery,"

"Good morning, Chief."

"Just heard that Dr. Payne has recovered enough to get back to his duties so he's planning to see to Mr. Morton tomorrow."

"Indeed." After a pause, "I've just come from Mrs. Clarendon's. I was able to confirm that she did know some Somervilles who lived in Oxford. Not much, I know. I may be reading too much into the conversation but she seemed to me to be evasive."

"I trust your insight, Mrs. Montgomery. She'll continue to be a person of interest. And ... I'm interviewing Mabel Merriweather this morning"

"Oh."

"It has to be done."

"Chief," she said with hesitation. "I haven't told you everything that might be pertinent to Mr. Morton's case."

"I see."

"At the Livingstone party, Charles and I overhead Mabel and Mr. Morton having words. She said something about 'veneered' and called him a 'thieving wretch' and then said something about it being inappropriate that he was giving Myrtle such expensive jewelry in addition to flinging out the assumption that the money for such jewelry was from questionable sources. But you know how she can be."

"Mmmm. Yes, I do. Well, thank you, Mrs. Montgomery. Is there anything else I need to know?" he asked, looking at her keenly.

"No," she said sheepishly. "Scouts honor."

"Alright. By the way, I've been meaning to tell you the name of the fellow Violet was seen talking to at a party while in Toronto."

"Yes, you said he was someone who deals in antique jewelry."

Chief Goodman put his car in gear, "Owns a number of jewelry stores in Toronto as a matter of fact—name is Foxe, David Foxe, I believe it is."

Chapter 16: A Basket, Some Broth and a Beetle

"And you will be certain of declaring our wondrous communiqué to your aunt—pardon me—your great aunt," enthused Mrs. Johnson.

"Yes," replied Alice.

Alice and George had been sent by their grandmother to buy more caramels and, having completed their commission, were edging towards the door of the Grocery Emporium. It had taken rather longer than expected to dish out a pound of caramels and accept payment for them because Mrs. Johnson was bursting with the news of Chamberlain's successful coup as she described it.

"Remember to highlight the prestigiousness of the law firm and thereby the honor bestowed on our Chamberlain for being hired."

"Yes, yes, by all means, we will share your joy with her," said Alice.

"Consider it done," said George, tugging surreptitiously on Alice's coat sleeve while pulling open the door.

"Good night!" exclaimed George, having gained the sidewalk. "What a to-do about being hired part-time as a clerk."

"Maybe it's more about him being vindicated. Remember how upset Aunt Dorothea said Mrs. Johnson was at his sudden and, in her eyes, secretive departure so soon after Christmas? So instead of the worst scenario she was imagining, of being chased by gangsters or whatever fantastical notion she had come up with, he was in fact heading to a job interview. Presumably he said nothing because he wasn't sure of the outcome. I think the extra income is readily welcomed."

"No doubt."

"Oh, I am glad to hear it," enthused Dorothea when, having returned home from Mrs. Clarendon's, she was told the news.

"You were suspecting him of stealing the brooch!" exclaimed Edith.

"I'm sorry to say it but, yes. I first overheard about this expected windfall at a Girl Guides' gathering and sadly thought only of the cashing in of your brooch."

"Nothing so dramatic, thankfully," said Alice.

"Any other suspects up your sleeve?" teased George.

"George, this is not a laughing matter," said Edith, reprovingly. "There are still townspeople not in the clear."

"About this and the murder," inserted Dorothea.

"Surely not," said Alice.

"I'm afraid so. Questions are still not entirely answered in reference to the Merriweather sisters, Fiona Clarendon and even Violet," explained Dorothea.

Alice stole a glance at George.

"Not Violet in regards to the murder, surely," exclaimed Alice.

"Not the murder, no," replied Dorothea.

"Personally, I don't see how this could be a small town job," George said evenly.

"Yes, Dianna," said Dorothea. Dianna was standing in the doorway.

"Mrs. White is wanting a word with you, ma'am."

"Thank you, Dianna. Excuse me everyone."

In the kitchen, Dorothea found Bill Wainfleet leaning against the door.

"You just tell her, Bill. You just tell Mrs. Montgomery," bristled Mrs. White, wiping her hands on her apron.

"Good morning, everyone. Tell me what, Mr. Wainfleet?"

"Well, an odd thing for sure, ma'am."

Mrs. White snorted.

"An odd thing?" questioned Dorothea.

"Yes, ma'am. Well, and if I wasn't looking down the track first thing this morning and admiring the sun sparkling up the snow when I sees a bigger glint. Thought I'd just meander down and sees what's what. At a safe time, mind you; I don't hold with playing chicken with trains. Anyways, I tromped down the track and there was the darndest thing just off to the side of the track. What do you think it was, Mrs. Montgomery?"

"I'm sure I can't imagine."

"Jars. Jars of broth, it turns out."

"My jars!" blurted Mrs. White indignantly.

"Jars of broth?"

"Jars of broth, sure as we're standing here. From where they were lyin' I figure someone chucked them from the train. They had a soft landing in the snow."

"Well, all I can say is that if that jumped up Gladys Cooper didn't want that broth, she needn't have taken it. You and Anna go ahead and enjoy it, Bill," steamed Mrs. White.

"Was there a basket?" asked Dorothea.

"Basket? No, no basket. Are you alright, Mrs. Montgomery?"

Dorothea had sat down abruptly in a wooden chair by the long kitchen table.

"Yes, oh yes. I'm just so taken aback. Why on earth would Gladys not want Mrs. White's fine broth?"

"Beats me," interjected Dilman, "but finders keepers, losers weepers, eh, Bill?"

Dorothea sat at her desk in the library, gazing blankly at the list of names she'd jotted down and mindlessly munching a square of cinnamon toast, properly buttered to the edges, when she heard the telephone ring in the hall and Dianna answer it.

"I'll just get her, Mrs. Pequegnant."

Dorothea was already rising from her desk when Dianna entered.

"Mary Pequegnant?"

"Yes, ma'am."

"Thank you, Dianna."

"Hello, Mary!"

"Dorothea, I'm sorry to impose on short notice but your sister's handbag is repaired and I wondered if I might come by with it ... now?"

"Yes, of course, but we can easily come and get it."

"I know, but I also have some ... information for Mrs. Heyer."

"Come ahead then. I'll have some tea ready."

Dorothea replaced the receiver slowly. *What on earth could Mary Pequegnant have to tell Edith?* she asked herself on the way to the kitchen.

"Mrs. White, Mary Pequagnant will be here shortly for an unexpected visit. Would it be possible to have a tea tray sent to the sitting room?"

"To be sure. Dilman, fill the kettle."

"Thank you, Dilman."

Dorothea smiled and left the kitchen.

Betty White turned to her husband.

"That is what my sainted mother called a thin smile. If it involves Mary Pequegnant, it'll be about that jewel. Trouble is a brewing."

Dilman returned to polishing the silver.

"All that's brewing, my girl, is tea and it's best we remember it."

Betty sniffed. "You wait and see."

Edith was reading in the library with her feet tucked up sideways in the overstuffed wing chair. Dorothea poked the small fire without looking at her and said brightly, "So Mary Pequegnant is popping by with your hand bag in a few minutes."

"Indeed. How kind. She needn't have bothered. I could easily get it or wait until Dilman collects the parcels."

"She said she also has some information for you."

"Information?"

"Yes."

"What kind of information?"

"She didn't say."

"Hmmm, intriguing."

"Mrs. White is putting together a tea tray. Shall we move to the sitting room?"

"By all means. I picked up that book George and Alice are reading, *The Great Gatsby* and I need a break from it. Good heavens, but that man is on a collision course!"

"What man?"

"Jay Gatsby."

"Oh."

When Mary Pequegnant walked into the sun-warmed sitting room, Dorothea felt a chill. She had known Mary long enough to recognize that clouded look on her face.

"Mary, come and sit. Edith, why don't you pour out for a change?"

Edith glanced at her sister with raised brows but picked up the teapot.

"Has Bertie recovered from his cold?" asked Dorothea, handing a plate of ginger cookies to Mary.

"Completely. Thankfully, as everyone seems to want their eyes examined. Annie Hacker came in for an appointment and said she thinks the new girl has much potential."

"I'm glad to hear that. What a weight lifted for her."

There was a pause. Mary Pequegnant swallowed her mouthful of tea, set her cup in its saucer and reached for the paper package on the seat beside her.

"Mrs. Heyer ..."

"Edith."

"Edith," said Mary, handing over the parcel, "here is your hand bag."

"You needn't have made a special delivery," replied Edith, smiling.

"Yes, yes I did. Please look inside the bag."

Dorothea bit into a cookie without tasting it, her eyes fixed on Edith's fingers.

Paper and string set aside, Edith held up the bag for examination.

"You've done a marvelous job! I would never know that it had been mended. Thank you."

"Look inside," repeated Mary.

Edith pulled open the mouth of the bag. She peered in. She lifted her head and blinked at Mary with astonishment.

"But ... but ... you've found it!"

She laughed and scooped the scarab brooch out of the bag.

"Where on earth was it?"

Dorothea set down her cookie and gazed at Mary who was looking troubled.

"It had slipped inside the lining. The weight and edges of the other decorations had disguised that it was there."

"Oh, you clever, clever woman!"

Edith leaned over the tea table and vigorously shook Mary's hand.

"Maybe too clever," Mary said.

"What do you mean?" asked Dorothea.

"Mrs. … Edith … I am so sorry to have to tell you this, but that pin is a fake. It's made entirely of paste."

The clock on the mantel over the electric fireplace ticked solemnly.

"Paste."

"Yes."

Tick … tock … tick … tock…

"How can they be paste?" Edith asked thickly.

Mary spread out her hands and shook her head.

Edith rose abruptly. "I must call Harold."

Dorothea and Mary sat silently: Dorothea, in shock, and Mary, unhappy at having such news to give.

George strolled in and stubbed out a cigarette.

"Just saw Big G. She seemed distracted. I hear there are cookies." He leant over the plate and stacked three in his hand.

Dorothea took a breath. "George, I know you call your grandmother, Big G, out of affection, but I also know she isn't fond of it. Right now, I think it would be best to show that affection in a different way. You see, Mrs. Pequagnant has found the beetle brooch but in so doing has discovered that it is a paste fraud."

"What?" gasped George. "That's not possible."

"Why not?"

"Because, because," he stammered, "Grandpapa knows gems. He would never be taken in by a fake.

There's some mistake here." He looked pointedly at Mary.

"No mistake. I wish there were."

"But, but," he spluttered. "Where's Alice? Does she know?"

Dorothea shook her head.

"I'll find her." He turned on his heel, stopped and looked at his handful of cookies. Turning back to the tea tray, he brushed his hands together over the empty plate. Pivoting, he strode out of the room, leaving Dorothea and Mary contemplating a pile of cookie crumbs.

Returned from her call, Edith reported, "The line was scratchy but I know undoubtedly that Harold said the brooch was not paste when he presented it to me."

"Of course it wasn't," blurted George.

"It must have been swapped, Gran, somewhere between London and here," reasoned Alice.

"Exactly when did Harold give you the brooch?" asked Dorothea.

"About a month before we came to you. It was a bon voyage gift."

"And did you wear it out in public before coming?"

"Yes, but only at a few small dinners. Oh, well, no, there was one quite large party—a Guy Fawkes event, so that would be have been November 5."

"But I remember you saying, Big … Gran, that that lot were half cut all night."

Edith smiled at her grandson. "I'm not sure I said it quite in that way, but you're right; there were a lot of intoxicated people there."

"The passengers on the ship could be considered," pointed out Alice, "although you did only wear it that one evening."

"It would be enough," said George, "for anyone with an eye to it."

"This changes everything. We've shifted from what seemed a spur-of-the-moment snatch to premeditated robbery," said Dorothea.

Edith agreed. "Harold is alerting the London police and banking and jewel circles."

"It's likely to be a London caper so Chief Goodman can lay off the Willowsdown folks," asserted George.

"Yes, I suppose he can," replied Dorothea. In her mind, a tail of a thought twitched. It was like a glimpse from the corner of an eye, but she just couldn't grasp that tail. She felt sure that if she could, it would lead her to some kind of conclusion.

With the revelation that the scarab in Edith's possession was only paste, the Willowsdown connection didn't make sense. And yet the question still remained—how is it that the Merriweather sisters were suddenly able to afford insurance premiums? And there was still the black and white evidence that Mrs. Clarendon had at least been in the company of Bertram Somerville, a man known to have handled Edith's brooch. Her head hurt. Where did she go from here? Then it came to her: Reverend Watkins! Of course. She recalled George's comment after the first Sunday service that he and Edith and Alice had attended.

"Jolly fellow that parson of yours," he had said.

"Interesting word choice," Charles had replied. "I wouldn't have thought of that myself but I think you've hit on something there."

"An abiding joy?" asked Alice.

"You mean he's always that way or is that a Sunday show?" continued George.

She herself had said, "If he were a tree and you cut a chunk from him, it would be imprinted with the stamp of joy that comes from the knowledge of comfort in great sorrow and the assurance that though all is wrong now it will one day be put right."

And that, she thought now, *is why he has such a vast network of friends, acquaintances and correspondents. Surely if he cast his net, someone could be caught who knew the Coopers.*

"I have an idea," she announced to the others who were still drooping over the latest development in the bejeweled beetle business. "I'll let you know how it works out," she said as she headed to the telephone.

"I've come at your urgent request," said a smiling Reverend Watkins, while handing over his hat and gloves.

"Yes, thank you," replied Dorothea. "Come into the parlor. This won't take long." They settled into chairs and she continued, "You see, Gladys Cooper, one of our housemaids, left our employ on Christmas Eve without leaving a forwarding address. I'm hoping with your wide circle of friends and acquaintances, perhaps someone will know the family. Something odd has occurred which makes me anxious to get a hold of her. I'm also going to alert Chief Goodman as I fear something may have happened to her."

"Yes, I think I might be able to help; I'll certainly give it a go. But my dear lady, whatever makes you think something may have happened to her?"

"Jars of broth."

"Pardon me?"

"When Gladys left she was given a basket with jars of canned beef broth. Mrs. White thought the broth might be of benefit to Gladys' ill mother. Mr. Wainfleet informed me that he found jars of broth beside the track looking very like they had been pitched from the train. The jars, mind you, but not the basket."

"I see, yes, I see. That is very strange. But it needn't mean something sinister. Nevertheless, I'll start asking around. Can you describe her to me?"

"I can do even better. We had a group picture taken at Christmas of everyone in the household; a memento of this special time with my sister. This is Gladys here."

Reverend Watkins perched his spectacles at the end of his nose and peered at the framed picture. He drew it closer to him. His eyes narrowed slightly and then widened. He extended his arm out and examined from a distance. He pulled the picture back to close range. He handed back the photograph.

"Do you remember two years ago when I took a sabbatical and spent time in Oxford and London?" he asked, returning his glasses to his vest pocket.

"Yes."

"At Oxford I met a father and daughter. They seemed … how should I put it … somehow not quite the people they presented to the world. I never could put my finger on it." He pinched his white beard between finger and thumb. "They were at Oxford because the father, late in life, was completing post graduate work. Last year, in a chatty letter from a friend, I heard that he had died. Other than that, I never thought of them again. Until now. The man's name was Bertram Somerville. His daughter's name was Margery. That Margery is the same young lady who is in this photograph. The person you know as Gladys."

"So you're saying this Gladys Cooper is a fraud," said Chief Goodman, glancing back and forth between Dorothea and Reverend Watkins.

"Without a doubt," replied the reverend.

"Well, I don't have much to go on, though having that photograph is a pretty piece of luck."

"Looking back," mused Dorothea, "Gladys' fussing over not wanting to be in the picture takes on a whole new meaning. I just thought she was being rather ridiculously bashful."

"I'll have to ask Bill Wainfleet some questions," remarked the chief.

"Dilman took Gladys—Margery—to the station Christmas Eve and he reminded me that the 5:00 p.m. is an eastbound train," offered Dorothea.

"True enough. Well, that's something anyway. Reverend, how about you offer up a prayer for direction. I'd be obliged."

"And I would be honored to do so. Heavenly Father, this young woman is lost in many ways. You know how she came to be in this situation and You know how to free her if she will let You. Whatever part You have for any of us to play, help us with Your direction and grace. In the name of Jesus, amen."

"That will set us off on the right track," said Dorothea. "Since Gladys is not Gladys, but the daughter of Bertram Somerville, seller of the pin to Harold, then recent events take on an entirely different look. Did she steal the brooch, realize it was a fake and then stuff it in Edith's bag? No, that doesn't make sense. Edith was wearing the brooch at the party. She must have swapped them when Edith first arrived."

"Why did she wait so long to leave town?" asked the chief.

"Let me do some digging and see who I can find who might be a link between your sister and Miss Somerville," said the reverend.

"There is one connection," offered Dorothea and, nodding to Chief Goodman, said, "The article I showed you with pictures of Mrs. Clarendon and Bertram Somerville. Thirteen years ago," she explained to Reverend Watkins, "Mrs. Clarendon traveled with a group of friends who were guests at various country homes in England and Scotland. Bertram Somerville was one of the group. I foolishly conjectured a connection between Fiona and the Merriweather sisters but with Gladys being Margery Somerville, there is the real possibility of collusion with Fiona Clarendon."

"And after each visit, an article of jewelry was stolen," continued the chief. "Always just brooches."

"Ah I see," said the reverend, pinching his beard.

"Now, Mrs. Montgomery, I know you've already approached Mrs. Clarendon indirectly about this case, but I really can't have you continuing in any inquiries. It's not likely Fiona Clarendon had anything to do with missing jewels from country estates nor is our case here likely to be dangerous but you never know."

"I understand. But surely a neighborly cup of tea with the reverend and Mrs. Clarendon can't hurt?" She tipped her head and smiled.

Chief Goodman rolled his eyes.

"I don't want to hear about any tea parties. I'm going to be needing that photograph."

Chief Goodman was not liking this day. He would have to have a chat with Fiona Clarendon but before that lay the even more odious task of questioning Mabel Merriweather. He had opted to speak with her at her home rather than at the police station. This time, as he drove up the lane, it was undoubtedly the figure of Mabel who was shoveling the front porch steps. He hardly even noticed Molly racing beside the car.

"Morning, Chief," Mabel called shortly from the porch.

"Morning, Mabel."

"You said you wanted to speak with me alone so I've sent Myrtle to the barn."

He tromped up the freshly shoveled steps.

"I take it this isn't a social call," said Mabel, eyeing him coolly.

"No it isn't."

"Well, come in."

Sitting stiffly in the front room, he glanced across the hall into the kitchen. He'd much rather be lounging amiably around that table. Coming to the point, he said, "You were seen in the vicinity of Morton's Funeral Services on the night of Hugh Morton's death and your fingerprints were found on the doorknob to the workroom in which his body was found."

"Is that so?"

"It is. Can you explain that?"

"I had planned on talking with him but in the end I didn't."

"But you did go to his workroom."

"I put my hand on the doorknob but I didn't go in."

"And what did you want to talk with him about?"

"Nothing that would make me want to kill him."

"I think you should know that at the Livingstone party, a conversation between you and Mr. Morton was overhead in which you mentioned," he flipped through his notes, "something about 'veneered' and called him a 'thieving wretch.' You also said it was inappropriate of him to give Myrtle such expensive jewelry and seemed to intimate that the money for said jewelry came from questionable sources."

Mabel was breathing quickly now and her brow was ominously furrowed.

"Who said such a thing?"

"A reliable source. Were you planning on continuing this conversation the night you visited him?"

Mabel sat red-faced and silent, her hands tightly clenched.

"Mabel, Miss Merriweather, I don't want to have to charge you with obstructing justice, never mind what else I may have to charge you with."

"I'll not say another word until in the presence of my lawyer."

"Alright. I'm not going to charge you right now as I have no place to put you what with Arthur Poole being in the cell. But I expect you and your lawyer at the station this afternoon. If you don't show, I'll have no alternative but to charge you with obstructing justice along with," he gulped, "murder."

"Chief Goodman. To what do I owe the privilege?" asked Fiona Clarendon as said man was directed to a chair.

He shook his head at the cigarette box held up for his selection and told himself that just because a woman smoked it didn't make her a jewel thief or a murderer. He knew he was an old-fashioned man and sharing a gasper with a woman just wasn't the thing and never could or would be as far as he could see.

She chose not to take one either and they eyed one another over the leather inlaid coffee table.

"I didn't see your name in my appointment book. Perhaps you are here to meet with Clarence?"

"Sorry to barge in on you, but it's you I need a word with."

"You didn't exactly barge in but I do only have a few minutes."

"Right you are. I think you should know that your fingerprints were found in Hugh Morton's apartment."

"Why shouldn't they be? I visited him last week."

"Were you on friendly terms with him?"

"Friendly enough."

"Friendly enough to visit him evidently. Was there a particular reason for the visit?"

"He wanted advice on a gift he was giving someone."

"Would this 'someone' be Myrtle Merriweather?"

"You're very quick, Chief Goodman. Yes, as a matter of fact."

"I see. Was this gift a piece of jewelry? A brooch perhaps?"

"Yes."

"Did he ask you because you have expertise in jewelry?"

"I like to think I'm a connoisseur."

"Was this a recently purchased piece?"

"It was one he had. He said it had been his mother's."

"I see. I need you to make a statement about this. When we're done here, if you'd be so kind as to give your statement to Joe North at the station."

"Is that really necessary?"

"Hugh Morton has been murdered, Mrs. Clarendon. It's necessary."

"Fine. Is that all?"

"Not quite." Removing Dorothea's framed photograph from a small briefcase, he said, "Cast your eye over this photograph if you would."

He watched her keenly as she studied the family/staff photograph from Mrs. Montgomery.

"Yes?"

"Just wondering who in that photograph you know."

She stared at him.

"Who I know? All of them. Really, Mr. Goodman."

"All of them, you say."

"Of course, all of them. I don't personally know Mrs. Montgomery's staff, naturally, but I recognize them. Well …" she squinted again at the picture, "except that one."

"Which one?"

She finger nailed Margery Somerville, alias Gladys Cooper.

"You don't know her?"

"Why ever should I?"

"It's just that she's the daughter of a friend of yours, a Bertram Somerville."

He caught the slight twitch of an eyebrow.

"I've never heard of a Bertram Somerville."

"That's very odd. How would you explain these pictures?"

From a file folder, he drew out the library newspaper article. He placed it on the coffee table, pinning it down with two fingers from each hand.

"Oh," she said coolly, scanning the headline and photos, "that Bertram Somerville. He was merely a fellow house guest."

"Sounds like you and your fellow house guests spent at least four months together."

He replaced the article.

Fiona Clarendon opened the cigarette box, chose one and lit it with unwavering smoothness.

"Well, yes, but there were others around with whom to get close. Does Clarence know you are here? Has he seen this?"

"No and no. Why would Margery Somerville come to Willowsdown?"

"It's a quaint town."

"With this picture, I should be able to track her down with fair ease. Perhaps then you could meet." He looked at her directly until she averted her eyes and blew smoke toward the ceiling.

"Until then, you will have to take my word that I do not know this Somerville girl and I had nothing to do with the thefts in that article. Nothing." She tapped her cigarette against the chrome ashtray. "I'm assuming a police questioning has somewhat the features of the confessional in that what has been said goes no further. I will certainly tell my husband whatever I think necessary, say what you will."

He had never had up close dealings with Mrs. Clarendon and had heard of her only as an elegant import from England. The chill he felt would have been out of place in summer but being the end of December, he figured it could be attributed to a draft and not the circumstance.

He stood.

"We'll each have to say what is necessary. Thank you for your time."

Chapter 17: A Light at the End of the Tunnel?

While Chief Goodman was engaged in his distressing rounds, Dorothea was at the library, settling herself into further newspaper investigation. She found Alice and Violet scrutinizing fashion advertisements and added her pile of back issues to theirs.

"Hello, Aunt Dorothea. Violet is trying to extrapolate from last year's fashions what might be the direction to take for new trends in hats and accessories."

"Good thinking. Any ideas?"

"Mmmm, some," said Violet, biting her lip deep in creative contemplation.

Dorothea picked up a sheet plastered over with advertisements; she was particularly struck by one featuring a woman approximately her age. She read the heading out loud, "Are grey-haired women honest?" She laughed, saying, "I would think the answer is obvious."

She leafed over a few pages.

Charges Crumble Like Egyptian Dynasties

Charges of fraud against Elizabeth and David Foxe were dropped today for lack of evidence. The couple were recently charged with selling paste replicas of Egyptian jewelry which they claimed to have come from recent archaeological digs. Evidence against them was conflicting and circumstantial and did not stand up in court. The couple own several prestigious jewelry stores in Toronto.

"Violet."

Violet looked up.

"Would this be the couple Ewan was staying with?"

Dorothea slid the paper with its picture and article across the table.

"Yes. Elizabeth and David Foxe." She scanned the article. "That's ridiculous. Sour grapes, I expect, from a disgruntled customer."

"Where did you meet them?"

"Eleanor and Chester Smith—you know—Olive's cousins, hosted a dinner party with a dance after. Ewan and the Foxes came to the dance."

"So Eleanor and Chester know the Foxes?"

"Know of them anyway. It was quite a posh affair. Lots of affluence and influence." She paused. "I did feel rather out of my depth but," she asserted, "those are entirely the kind of people I hope to see on the other side of my workplace counter."

"Quite."

"Olive, how can I get in touch with your cousins, Eleanor and Chester?"

A startled Olive removed her headset and peered at a slightly puffing Dorothea.

"I know their number but it's long distance."

"I know, dear. Do you think they would be willing to host two people on very short notice?"

"Well, I don't know."

"Could you ask? On my behalf? It's rather urgent. Two people arriving this afternoon. Call me at home when you know something. Thank you ever so much," she called as she bustled out the exchange office door.

"Edith, I need you to have an accident in front of Mrs. Clarendon's house."

"Dorothea, whatever are you babbling about?"

"You must pretend to sprain an ankle or something so that you have to impose on her. It's her at-home day."

"Why?"

"I need information and I know you can charm it out of her. I'm taking George to Toronto, otherwise I would give it a whirl."

Edith's eyes sparkled and narrowed.

"What sort of information?"

"Charles, it's the only way. We all need to act before it's too late. Please have your friend at the shipping line look up the rosters of all passenger ships within the last six to twelve months. For the other names I gave you, have him check as far back as 1923. Tell him we need this as soon as possible."

"Chief Goodman isn't going to like this and I'm not sure I do either."

"Chief Goodman or the Toronto police would be obvious. George and I can do this with nary a wonder."

"You're a wonder all right," he said and kissed her hand.

From the meeting with Reverend Watkins and the chief, to the epiphany at the library, through rallying the troops, to boarding the train, just over two hours had elapsed. George was rummaging through the lunch basket Mrs. White had frantically pulled together. All of the household was charged and poised for action although none of them knew to what outcome. Dorothea leaned back in her seat and closed her eyes. She thought of Reverend Watkins' statement, "somehow not quite the people they presented to the world." She hoped she was right in her notions because if so, that was the linchpin. If not, she would look a blithering idiot.

"Sandwich, Aunt Dot?"

"Yes, thank you."

They ate in silence, both deep in thought.

"So, what ho, Aunt? We're charging off to Toronto and I've no idea why."

"To remove masks and connect dots."

"That's pretty cryptic."

Cryptic. In her mind a pinpoint of light flashed onto what seemed to be a conclusive theory, but she couldn't get her brain to spread the light to see it in its fullness. She blinked and it was gone.

"Well?"

"Did Elizabeth and David Foxe know Gladys … Margery Somerville? Did Margery have them make a copy of Edith's brooch?"

"How would Margery know Gran would have it?"

"She would have seen it when she unpacked Edith's trunks. And Edith didn't wear it right away."

"But Margery couldn't have known that. It would have been too risky to take it and send it and wait for the copy."

"Very true. But there must be some connection."

"You mean swap when Eleanor and Chester Smith came for the party?"

"Possibly. Or Fiona Clarendon *does* know Margery and they colluded."

"If that's the case, the real beetle could be anywhere."

Dorothea sat thinking. "I must send a telegram to the postmaster when we get to Union Station."

"Right," said George with a bemused look.

By sheer good fortune, or maybe not so good, Edith had in fact slipped on the ice as she approached the

Clarendon home. She and Alice were trying to appear as nonchalant strollers which, as Edith said, was preposterous in the first place; only in Canada would people face such cold on purpose merely for a refreshing promenade. Her mind was furiously working on how she could fake a fall when the next thing she knew, she was looking up at Alice from the frozen ground. Nothing was sore except her bottom but getting up from a real fall made it easy to produce a fake limp.

"We're for it now, my girl," said Edith as she phonily limped up the Clarendon walk and Alice phonily supported her.

"We can do this, Grandmamma," urged Alice encouragingly.

"You're right. The worst that can happen is she'll think we're lunatics." She grinned mischievously.

A young woman in uniform with lowered eyes answered the door.

"Thank goodness someone is home!" blurted Alice. "My grandmamma has taken a spill and seems to have badly twisted her ankle. Would it be possible to have a sit down and ring my aunt's house?"

"Oh, oh, I think I think that should be fine," stammered the girl. "Although I'm not sure, I'm not sure which room to put you in ..."

"I can rest here," cut in Edith, limping over to a very upright hallway chair, "while you find Mrs. Clarendon. That way you'll know just where to put us." She beamed kindly at the flustered girl.

"Yes, thank you, I'll do that." She bobbed and hurried away.

"We're in," breathed Alice.

A few fidgety minutes later, and then they heard heels clacking over the marble tiles of the rather vast front hall.

"So sorry to impose," began Edith before Fiona Clarendon had a chance to say anything. "Silly of me. Alice and I were out for a walk and I slipped on a patch of ice. My ankle is throbbing dreadfully. Perhaps a sit down and a cup of tea while we wait for Dilman to fetch us?"

"Certainly, no trouble at all," cooed Mrs. Clarendon. "You must come in and put your foot up. I'll have the girl fetch up some ice to keep down the swelling and then bring in some tea."

Edith stood and winced, pretending pain in her ankle but, in fact, grimacing at the thought of ice packed where there was no reason to pack it.

"May I use your telephone to ring Aunt Dorothea?" asked Alice, nodding to the instrument on a corner table.

"Go right ahead. I will get your grandmother settled."

Once the prerequisite fussing was accomplished and the ice dutifully packed around her ankle, Edith looked around Willowsdown's first modern house.

"You've been to Paris? I recognize the unique styling."

"Yes, I was there two years ago and kept the ideas in my head. We finished building just last year."

"I read somewhere that this styling has been give a name—art deco, I think," offered Alice. "By the way, Grandmamma, Dilman will be here soon but not immediately."

"Ah, he's a good man is Dilman. Those are the ones one wants to hold onto, wouldn't you say, Mrs. Clarendon?"

"Yes, quite."

"For my part," said Alice, "I find so often there are those you wish would leave on their own accord rather than having to let them go."

"One can't just let staff go willy nilly, dear. One must consider the ramifications for all involved."

"Well," sniffed Alice, "seems to me so many of them nowadays think they are too good for service so I say let them find the green grass they are looking for."

Fiona Clarendon had been resting back in her squared off tiger print chair, but now uncrossed her ankles and leaned forward.

"I have never kept a servant who looked me in the eye; far too familiar. The other day one of the new ones handed me my newspaper directly without putting it on a tray."

Alice tsked. "Did you sack her?"

"Not yet. She's very new and lately it seems there has been a revolving door of help. So tiresome. I'm waiting to see how she works out."

Just then, the girl who had admitted them carried in the tea tray. Mrs. Clarendon raised an eyebrow at Alice and nodded towards the girl, acknowledging the presence of the trayless newspaper culprit.

"I think the ice has done the trick," said Edith. "What is your name?"

"Esther, ma'am."

"Esther, if you would be so kind to take it with you," said Edith warmly.

A somewhat frosty silence followed the girl's exit as Mrs. Clarendon poured out the tea.

"Nothing like a cuppa as the working classes say. She seems quite capable," remarked Edith.

"You'd say that about anyone, Grandmama. You are too soft."

"That sort of attitude can easily lead to lax service and things going missing," said Fiona Clarendon pointedly.

"Precisely. You and Aunt are the same. That's very likely how Gladys got away with your brooch."

"Yes, but, my dear, Gladys was not who she said she was. An entirely different circumstance."

"No, it isn't. If Aunt Dorothea was more discerning and less ready to believe a hard luck story, Gladys would never even have gained admittance to the household."

"Please forgive us, Mrs. Clarendon, this is an ongoing family feud," said Edith apologetically.

"Not at all. I must say I agree with your granddaughter. Margery Somerville might be good at disguises but she's not that good."

"Well, I certainly wish Aunt Dorothea had been aware that you knew Margery and all this could have been averted. But then you would have had no reason to see Margery. How long have you known her? Has she always been a thief? I'm sorry. She couldn't have been a thief always if she's someone you've known," enthused Alice.

Edith snorted involuntarily changing it to a sort of sneeze.

"Excuse me. I hope I'm not catching a chill."

"Her father was a friend of mine for a few years but they left for Egypt some years after the war and I lost touch," explained Mrs. Clarendon.

"What took them to Egypt?" asked Alice.

"He was interested in archaeology and connected himself with some dig or other."

"It really is thrilling, isn't it? Grandmama and I stayed at Highclere a few years back after the King Tut find."

The door opened.

"Yes," snapped Fiona Clarendon.

"The driver is here, ma'am, for the ladies."

"Ah good. I was just thinking we were overstaying our welcome. Come, Alice, my ankle is feeling better already. We musn't keep Dilman waiting."

Chapter 18: Taking It to the Big City

At Union Station, Dorothea sent her telegram to Willowsdown's post office while George called DeLuxe Taxicabs.

Settled in the cab, Dorothea said, "Now, George, no matter how you feel about the Smiths whisking Violet away, I need you to be at your most pleasant."

"No worries there; that's all over. I tip my hat to Violet and her new career in the glitter and glam of Toronto."

"I hope that wasn't a sneer, George Albert. London may have its cosmopolitan polish but it has its decidedly smeary side too."

"I know it and I meant no disparagement."

She smiled at him. "You're a good man, George. Now to work. Let's review the plan."

"Righto. I'm a man about town wanting the best that Canada has to offer in jewelry to take back as a souvenir and gift to my ladylove. Heard of Foxe's Jewels. Heard that the Smiths know them. Have briefly met the Smiths who hosted hometown girl, Violet. Thought they could hook me up with said Foxes for a private showing. When with the Foxes, I weasel out any info I can."

"And I, as the twittering elderly relation, do the same. I do hope for Olive's sake, and for Violet's, for that matter, that the Smiths are not involved."

At Willowsdown's police station, Joe North was stopped mid-bite into his sandwich when the door burst open and banged against the wall. Myrtle Merriweather bounded in.

"Where's Chief Goodman?" she demanded.

"Not exactly sure, ma'am. May I help you?"

"No, you may not. I assume you're expecting him in?"

"Sure, at some point. He may have stopped at home for a mouthful of dinner."

"Well, I'll wait," she huffed.

"Let me show you into his office. There's a chair here you can use while you wait. Uh, may I get you a coffee or something?"

In a calmer voice, she replied, "No thanks, Joe. I'll be fine." She suddenly noticed Arthur Poole in the cell. "What are you doing here?"

Being the well-mannered young man that he was, Arthur stood up when Myrtle addressed him and looked across the room to Joe.

"Um, he's remanded in custody on the charge of murdering Hugh Morton," explained Joe.

"What? But that's ridiculous. How many people do you think killed him? Chief Goodman also has my sister down as a suspect!"

"Please, Miss Merriweather, if you could just sit down. The chief will be here soon. It'll all get sorted out."

Myrtle looked back and forth between the young men and then exhaled deeply seeming to crumple just a little.

"Yes, all right."

She slumped down onto the battered armchair; Arthur returned to sitting on the cot in the cell and Joe perched on a stool behind the front counter. There was silence in the station.

The front door opened slowly and Mrs. Poole stepped inside, holding a pie.

"Ma!" uttered Arthur and stood up from his cot.

"Afternoon, Mrs. Poole," said Joe.

Myrtle Merriweather and Lillian Poole nodded to each other, exchanging the look that women all over the world who have suffered recognize.

Joe came out from behind the counter, carrying the stool. "You can sit on this, Mrs. Poole." He placed it in front of the cell.

"Thank you, Joe. Arthur, I made a pie from the cherries I put down this summer."

Arthur gulped and blinked back tears. "Thanks, Ma."

"Here, let me take that from you, Mrs. Poole," said Myrtle. "Joe, move the armchair over to the cell and I'll sit on the stool. You must have some dishes and cutlery here."

"On a shelf behind the counter," puffed Joe as he muscled the armchair out of the office.

Myrtle placed the pie on the counter and peeked around to find the shelf with the dishes and cutlery. The door was pushed opened briskly and Mrs. Clarendon strode in.

She cast her eyes over the room and announced to Joe, "Chief Goodman would like you to take my statement."

"Right, Mrs. Clarendon. I'll just be a minute."

"Is there a place I can sit down?" she asked.

"Ah, well, I guess you could sit in Chief Goodman's chair," replied Joe. "Let me get it out from behind his desk." Leaving the armchair in front of the cell, he carried the stool back behind the counter for Myrtle to sit on. While Mrs. Clarendon tapped her foot, he rolled the chief's swivel chair to the other side of the desk.

"I'll get you a pen and paper. If you'll write down your statement, I'll read it and sign off on it."

Meanwhile, Myrtle and Mrs. Poole had found plates and forks and a knife with which to slice the pie.

"Do you mind if Joe has a piece?" whispered Myrtle.

"Not at all. He's just doing his job," replied Mrs. Poole.

Mrs. Poole cut two large wedges. She carried one to Arthur.

"Joe," she said, standing in front of the cell. "I can't get the plate through the bars."

"Oh. Right. Ummm, let me get the key."

"This is for you, Joe," said Myrtle pointing to the piece of pie.

"Great. Thanks."

He unlocked the cell door, Mrs. Poole handed over the pie, and Joe relocked the door.

Mrs. Poole sat on the armchair by the cell door. Inside the cell was a straight backed caned chair which Arthur pulled over to be opposite his mother.

"Ma," he said under his breath, "I forgot to mention that the night Mr. Morton was killed, I had taken a jog around the block to clear my head. Did you say anything about that?"

Before an answer was forthcoming, Mabel Merriweather and her lawyer, along with a gust of snow, swirled in. Joe was just in the act of raising a forkful of pie to his mouth and so appeared to be standing around with his mouth hanging open. Which, when he saw two more people entering the station, was exactly how he felt.

"What on earth?" asked Mabel. "Why is everyone here? Where's Chief Goodman?"

"I'm a busy man," asserted the lawyer. "Chief Goodman stressed that my client needed to be here this afternoon and she is. I can't be waiting around all day."

"Myrtle, what are you doing here?" asked Mabel.

"I came to give Chief Goodman a piece of my mind."

"Joe," said Arthur from behind his bars, "it looks like you're needing more seats. You can have this chair." He rose from his seat at which moment Chief Goodman finally arrived.

"Chief Goodman!" declared Mrs. Clarendon and the lawyer at the same time.

"Chief Goodman," continued the lawyer, "Miss Merriweather is here as you requested."

"So I see. Thanks for being so prompt, Mabel ... Miss Merriweather. We'll need the privacy of the office. Mrs. Clarendon, if I could get you to finish your statement here at the counter...."

"It's hardly private," complained Mrs. Clarendon.

"I can set you up here in this far corner," suggested Joe. "The stool is tall enough for you to sit at the counter and write. Miss Merriweather, do you mind?" he asked, turning to Myrtle who had been surreptitiously eating pie perched on the stool.

"Not at all," she mumbled.

"You'll need this chair back," offered Mrs. Poole.

"And you can use this one," said Arthur, restating the offer of his chair.

Chief Goodman stood in the middle of his station pondering this dance of chairs.

"Joe, give me the cell key please."

"Righto."

Unlocking the cell, the chief said, "Mrs. Poole, if you don't mind visiting in here with Arthur, the two of you can sit on his cot. There's room on it too for you Myrtle if you want to sit down. I won't lock the cell," he reassured with a smile. He picked up the caned chair and nodded to the armchair, "Joe, do you mind bringing that back to the office? Now," he continued, carrying the caned chair, "who was here first?"

"I was," piped up Myrtle. "But since Mabel is here, I'll wait until you've finished with her."

"Thank you. Mrs. Clarendon, I leave you in the capable hands of Joe."

Mrs. Clarendon sniffed but didn't look up from her writing.

The swivel chair was rolled back to its place behind the desk and the armchair and caned chair were settled in front. The chief was making space on his desk for taking notes, the lawyer was shuffling papers, and muttering, "… highly irregular," Mabel was sitting rigidly, and Mrs. Poole and Myrtle, having helped themselves to pie, were carrying their plates into the cell to take a seat on the cot when the door opened…again. It revealed a white-haired, stooped gentleman—the town's doctor.

"You've got quite a party here, Joe!" laughed Dr. Payne, taking in the unlikely scene. "Can't say I remember there ever being a social gathering at the police station."

"Well …" Joe stopped, not knowing quite what to say.

"It's good to see you up and about again, doctor," said Myrtle from the cot in the cell.

"Thank you, Myrtle. It's good to be up and about. I see the chief is busy," he said to Joe. "I think it best that you interrupt. He's going to want to hear what I have to say. In fact, by the looks of it, everyone here is going to be interested in what I have to say."

Joe tapped on the glass of the office door, opened it and stuck in his head. "The doctor says I should interrupt you."

The chief was rubbing his bald head and looked relieved at an excuse to leave.

"Good to see you, doctor," he said, holding out his hand to meet the doctor's in a handshake. "What can I do for you? Wasn't actually expecting to see you until tomorrow. Did I forget to fill in some kind of form?"

"No, no, nothing like that. I'm feeling better and figured you'd want to make headway on Morton's case. I've just come from finishing the autopsy."

"I see. Maybe we should head over to your office. Things are a bit tight here as you can see," he grimaced.

"Not at all. What I have to say will clear everything up and put everyone right where they should be. Having this group on the spot here will save you time. I don't suppose there's a chair to sit on. I'm feeling much better but still definitely weak."

"You're welcome to mine, doctor," offered Mabel, eyeing him narrowly. She lifted it out of the office and placed it in front of the counter.

"Right. Ohhh, that feels better," he sighed, lowering himself into the chair. "I'm decidedly not quite the thing yet." He closed his eyes while the others stood or sat with bated breath, staring at him as if they could bore into his brain and extract what—it seemed—he was taking so long to tell.

"Ah, doc, could I get you a glass of water or something?" asked Joe tentatively.

"No, no, I'm fine. Just took a second to ease these old bones. Now, Mr. Morton." He steadily regarded each one in the room. "Mr. Morton was not murdered."

A communal gasp seemed to suck the air from the room followed by a babble of voices.

The thought sparked through the chief's mind that perhaps he should ring up Mrs. Payne for confirmation that her husband was, in fact, in recovery.

"But," he began.

The doctor held up a hand. "I know—all the extenuating circumstances made it look as though he'd been killed. Let me explain. You found Mr. Morton in a closed casket with another casket leaning against its lid. You noted a cut on his head. Is that right?"

Chief Goodman nodded.

"The autopsy showed that he'd had a heart attack. Without a doubt that is what killed him. Your report mentioned a pair of scissors in the casket. My thinking is that Morton was working on something in the casket. He suffered a heart attack and the spasms that accompanied it caused the lid of the casket to drop and the leaning casket to fall against it."

"Arthur, was there a casket leaning against the open one on the stand where we found Mr. Morton?" asked the chief.

"Yes, sir, there was. I helped Mr. Morton move it that morning. I don't know why he wanted it there. But it was there."

"But what about the abrasion?" the chief questioned.

"If you recall, there was no blood," replied Dr. Payne. "My guess is again because of the spasms, he hit his head against the side of the casket even as he died."

"Arthur, the scissors found in the casket ... was there another pair at the funeral home?" asked the chief.

"Not that I ever saw."

"So you would have handled them on occasion?"

"Not often but, yes, I did."

"What you're saying. doctor," said Chief Goodman contemplatively, "is that Mr. Morton died of natural causes but because he did some flailing about, the lid of one casket closed and another one, that had been leaning against it, pinned it shut making it look as though he'd been deliberately knocked into the casket."

"That's how I read it," stated Dr. Payne.

Everyone in the room was silent. Mrs. Poole slowly stood up from the cell cot. "So you're saying that while he was caught up in one of his cheating schemes he was struck dead? He was likely using those scissors in some hoodwinking trick with the lining."

"I make no suppositions as to what he was doing," said the doctor gravely, "I'm only reporting the facts of his cause of death."

"'No suppositions'!" snorted Mabel. "Suppositions nothing! Don't be such an ass, doctor. Of course he was doing something nefarious."

The doctor shook his head but couldn't keep from smiling.

"Well! Well! Well, this is an unlikely turn of events!" burst out the chief. "I'm not sure what to say besides—you're all free to go and ... is there anymore of that pie I've been smelling?"

The lawyer and Mrs. Clarendon did not stay to enjoy the compact pieces that Mrs. Poole was able to eke out of the remainder of the pie. And the doctor, even after being the messenger of such good news, was, with his recent illness, not yet up to indulging in pie. But the others, with the freedom of merriment that comes after a time of constricting gloom and anxiety, felt they were feasting royally.

"I feel like laughing and laughing," said Mabel. "It seems too good to be true! Seems like true justice has been served!"

"And you do understand I was just doing my job," said the chief.

"I know and I knew it. But it's hard nonetheless to be accused or at least suspected of something so wicked as murder even if it was Hugh Morton," replied Mabel.

"Mabel!" exclaimed Myrtle reprovingly.

"Do you mind if I tell the chief now what I didn't want to say without a lawyer present?" Mabel asked Myrtle.

A rosiness suffused Myrtle's face. "Might as well."

"I did call Hugh Morton a thieving wretch at the Livingstone's party. A few days before the party it was made clear to me that Hugh Morton had cheated the Austen family on the casket their little one was buried in. When I saw him at the party, I was livid. Who could do such a thing? On top of that, he'd been courting Myrtle to my disgust and had in the last two months given her three obviously, even to my eyes, expensive brooches."

"Mabel was furious that I even accepted them," inserted Myrtle. "I wasn't thrilled at being called on by Mr. Morton but when he presented me with the first brooch it seeded an idea. With the second brooch, the idea came to fruition."

"But she wasn't telling me and I couldn't understand what on earth she saw in the man; she knew what he'd been doing to community people! I did go that night to tell him in no uncertain terms that he'd better stay away from Myrtle or I'd be sure to find a way to bring to light his thieving ways."

"And how did you plan to go about doing that?" asked the chief dryly.

"No idea," said Mabel shortly. "And that's why I turned around at the workroom door and went home never having seen him. After you told me about my fingerprints and the overheard conversation, I realized I was in a precarious position."

"In the meantime, we'd had the brooches appraised and then sold to give us some cash flow," broke in Myrtle. "I figured if Mr. Morton wanted to give me jewelry, I'd let him keep courting me and get what I could out of him. Thieving wretch."

The chief barked with laughter, Joe's guffawing caused him to choke on his mouthful of coffee and Arthur stood and bowed to the sisters. Mrs. Poole, who more than all of them had a reason to feel giddy with freedom, was glad, glad, glad but, unlike the sisters, was not ready to share the full extent of that gladness.

She knew she needed to, not keep Adam's being alive a secret, but she wasn't there yet. She hoped that someday she would be brave enough. It did feel good that there were at least two others who knew the truth. What they thought about it—and her—was not important to her right now. Her Arthur was free now on many levels. He would make a fine funeral director. With Mr. Morton now needing burial he would have to learn fast.

In a house near Chestnut Park in the Rosedale suburb of Toronto, Chester Smith paced the floor of the front sitting room. Eleanor was due home from work any minute. He hoped for an opportunity to speak with her before their guests arrived. He had left a message at her work but there was always the chance that she hadn't received it. If she hadn't, then the unexpected meeting with two people from Willowsdown might prove awkward.

Footsteps along the hall and then Eleanor in the room.

"Florence said you would be in here."

She thumped down in a chair and vigorously rubbed her eyes.

"What a day! I think I didn't look up from my typewriter once. Did I hear Florence say she would be bringing tea in here? Whatever for?"

"We're expecting guests from Willowsdown: not Violet."

Eleanor stopped rubbing her eyes.

"No! I never imagined they would actually face us down. Are you sure?"

"Olive called to say that there would be two guests coming in this afternoon and her understanding was that it was a matter of urgency."

"Lots of people come to town that doesn't mean it has anything to do with ..."

"But why come to us?" he broke in.

"Well," began Eleanor when the doorbell sounded. They looked at each other. "Just be friendly and breezy and assume it has nothing to do with anything we've done."

"Thank you so much for indulging us," gushed Dorothea. "George here has been so persistent about finding the perfect piece and has scorned everything at home so I finally threw up my hands and said, 'Fine! We'll go to the city right this minute.'"

"Good of you to take us in on short notice what? Violet speaks highly of you so it seemed we'd be sure to find hospitality for strangers. The proverbial hosting of angels and all that, what?" blithered George.

"No trouble at all," replied Chester smoothly.

"You'll need to stay the night of course," said Eleanor somewhat stiffly.

"Yes, I think we will. It was a last minute decision so it has put us into town rather late," said Dorothea.

"I'm looking to hunt up the Foxes of Egyptian jewelry fame," remarked George. "Violet says you know them. She was introduced at a party here. Hoping you could arrange a private showing with them and their loot, eh what?"

"I'm afraid our acquaintance with them is rudimentary but I can certainly put a word in for you," offered Chester.

"You'd best ring them now, Chester, if you hope to catch them at work. I work as head secretary at Pruitt, Pruitt and Hewitt Legal Firm a block from the Foxes' main store so I have an idea of their hours," explained Eleanor.

"A legal firm, how interesting," commented Dorothea warmly.

"Yes, interesting enough that I plan to go into law myself."

"What? To become a lawyer?" asked George, incredulous.

Dorothea gave a little cough. "I'm sorry; a tickle in my throat. Another cup of tea would *be so pleasant*, George," said Dorothea crisply, enunciating her last words.

"Right. Right you are, aunt. Good show, Miss Smith, one always likes to know of a lawyer with integrity," said George, passing Dorothea's empty cup to Eleanor who was pouring.

"What kind of law are you thinking of practicing? Thank you, George," said Dorothea, as he handed back her refilled cup.

"Criminal," replied Eleanor looking hard at George.

"You'll never want for work eh what? People bashing people over the head, blackmail, stealing of whats-its of all sorts."

"Chester, be sure to make that call," broke in Eleanor.

"I'm off, " he said bolting from his chair.

The exit of Chester shifted the conversation to dribblings about the weather that managed to stretch out until his return.

"They'll be available tomorrow morning at 11:00," he announced.

"Oh jolly good," said George beaming convincingly.

Before supper, Dorothea received the expected reply from her telegram to Willowsdown's post office.

"No parcels coming or going," she read. "One telegram received."

Before retiring to bed a telegram arrived from Charles: M.S. arrived November 11.

"Night, Ches."

"Night, El."

"By the way, do you remember this George as being such a nitwit?"

"No. For that matter, I don't recall the aunt as being so provincial."

"I don't think we have anything to worry about."

"I hope you're right."

Chapter 19: Dramatic Deductions

"They're rather pleasant types," commented George.

"Yes, they are. Before you came down I acted on a hunch and peppered them with some tricky questions."

Dorothea and George were finishing coffee, their hosts having decamped to places of business, leaving them with warm wishes for the success of their day.

"What questions?"

"Never mind about that right now. Suffice it to say that I've made some changes to our plans. You'll begin on your own with the Foxes. I need to attend to some critical telegrams and cables."

Eleanor had left Dorothea with detailed directions to the jewelry store and the telegraph office. The streetcar deposited tm at a corner, and they each strode down separate blocks: George sauntering away, swinging a walking stick and Dorothea stepping briskly.

She easily found the C.P.R. office. Pushing open the door to staccato tapping by the telegraph operators was reassuring. Such industry would surely produce results. At the counter she dashed off a message to Edith. The cable to Edith's husband, Harold, was trickier. She tapped her teeth with the pencil. She needed precise information. She needed it quickly. And she needed it from two fronts. She thought. She wrote. She handed it to the operator. Then on her second hunch for the day, she sent a telegram to Mary Pequegnant.

George too had found his building. He, however, did not walk into audible occupation but hushed enterprise.

The carpet quieted his footsteps. The glass counters gleamed beckoningly but were actually transparent stop signs. An older man with black and grey hair stood behind the counter directly facing the door. His face was a triangular shape with a grey and white beard clipped closely around his mouth.

"Ah, you must be Mr. Seyler," he said, smiling expansively, moving out from behind the counter with an outstretched hand.

"Spot on, old chap," said George, transferring his walking stick to the left and shaking hands. "And you are Mr. Foxe; pleased and all that." *Good heavens,* thought George. *I've heard that people can look like their dogs but never heard they could look like their names.*

"I'm afraid that my wife won't be able to be with us," said Foxe. "I understood you were to be accompanied by someone else?"

"Right, my aunt—well, great aunt to be precise. She'll be toddling along anytime now. Important to get a woman's point of view in these matters, what? Want to be sure to pick the thing that will dazzle the sweetheart, eh?"

George resisted the temptation to twirl his stick. That just might be gilding the lily.

"Precisely, sir. I've laid out a selection of our finest in Egyptian styling. Mr. Smith mentioned that was your particular interest."

"Too true. The old bean is absolutely batty about all things Pharaoh. Seems all the girls are."

"It does seem that way."

"I was just flapping the gums with Mrs. Clarence Clarendon for pointers, you know. She's a connoisseur by all accounts. I'm sure she comes to check your wares."

Mr. Foxe considered.

"It's possible she's been to one of our stores, but I can't recall serving someone by that name myself."

"By Jove, those are dazzlers!" exclaimed George whose eye had caught a pair of earrings.

The door bell jangled and two women entered. Mr. Foxe nodded to the young woman who had been dusting tea services. She greeted the customers and, setting down her duster, moved off to dance attendance on them.

"Our dangling beetle earrings," continued Mr. Foxe. "A stunning setting of emeralds, lapis lazuli, gold and diamonds."

The door opened again. This time Dorothea crossed the threshold.

"Right ho, Aunt," called George, "what do you think of these?"

"Just one second, George. You must be Mr. Foxe. So pleased to meet such a celebrated jeweler," enthused Dorothea, holding out her hand.

Mr. Foxe took her hand and George said, "Mr. Foxe, may I introduce you to Mrs. Dorothea Montgomery, my great aunt. So Aunt Dot, pretty spiffy, eh what?"

"They are extraordinary," agreed Dorothea, leaning over the glass counter.

"I've only begun running my eye over 'em all," said George.

"You have an outstanding collection here, Mr. Foxe. It must have taken some time to put it together."

"We began with a few pieces after the war and have been adding to them ever since."

"Are they all from actual digs?" Dorothea asked breathlessly.

"Oh no. Many are but we design just as many ourselves."

"How do you know how to make them with such an authentic look?"

"We receive sketches from time to time."

"They are stunning. I see why you are the place to come to. How exciting to have direct archaeological contact! George, here, of course, has seen Lord Carnarvon's collection. I think it would be thrilling to be a part of such discoveries! The closest I have come is by hosting my young friend, Ewan MacMurray. I believe you know Ewan and his father. Oh dear, I can't think of his name ... Thomas, Timothy, Hezekiah, no no, don't be absurd, Dorothea ... Albert maybe ..."

"I believe it's Edmund," broke in Mr. Foxe, a touch impatiently.

"Edmund, that was it, eh what, Aunt? Good show old fellow! She would have gone on and on had you not brought it to mind."

"I only just remember, though I'm not sure why. We've really had no connection with that dig—well, er, with any specific digs," said Mr. Foxe with a noticeably blanched face.

Dorothea had wandered over to another case.

"Mr. Foxe, this is a most unusual piece."

She pointed to an almost oval brooch topped with a small replica of England's coronation crown. In the center of the brooch was a large sapphire surrounded by diamonds and pearls and surrounding that was a band intricately patterned with diamonds, amethysts, emeralds, rubies and sapphires. The crown itself sparkled with tiny diamonds and rubies.

"You have a good eye, Mrs. Montgomery. I created that in 1920 to celebrate 10 years of the king's reign."

"How magnificent! I must have it!"

"Oh, ah. I'm so sorry. I should have removed it earlier. I actually received confirmation this morning that another customer has decided to purchase it."

His employee looked over in surprise.

"Oh I am disappointed. Perhaps you will make another one?"

"I had been thinking latterly that I would begin designing another piece for what will hopefully mark the twentieth anniversary of the reign and not make anymore of these once this one sold."

Beads of sweat were breaking out on the jeweler's brow.

Dorothea lifted an eyebrow at George which was the pre-arranged signal that their work there was done.

"Well, I've had a good look 'round," spouted George. "Just wrap up those beetle danglers, would you? That's a good fellow. Here's my card. You can send the bill there."

The phone rang.

"It's for you, Mr. Foxe."

"Thank you, Doris. Be so kind as to wrap these for Mr. Seyler." Picking up the phone, he listened briefly. "Ah, Mr. Smith. Yes, they are; they're just leaving. Would you like to speak to one of them? No? An invitation? … something of interest? Certainly. As it happens tomorrow evening will suit just fine. Thank you. Until then."

His sangfroid restored, Mr. Foxe escorted Dorothea and George to the door and bid them good day.

"Whew!" exclaimed George. "That buzzed along. Did you get anything?"

"More than I expected. We'll gather our bags from the Smiths' house and head to the station. I need to order my thoughts on the train. I can tell you more later. By the way, you were superb."

George blushed as he reached for his cigarette case.

Chapter 20: The Weaving of Threads

Back at home, Dorothea, Edith and Alice were in the library toasting themselves before a fire, each with their feet tucked up into their ample chairs.

"Wouldn't mother be shocked to see us sitting like this rather than with our ankles neatly crossed," observed Dorothea, gazing into the flames.

"She would indeed," agreed Edith, "bless her heart."

"I'm still flabbergasted at what you tell me about Hugh Morton," said Dorothea, returning to the news that was on the lips of everyone in town: the natural, rather than murderous death, of Mr. Morton. "And so Arthur is now our funeral director and the one who will be burying the man responsible for so much grief to his family. Goodness. Poetic justice."

"In what way?" asked Alice.

"Sorry, dear, I was musing out loud what should have been kept in my head. Bad habit. It's a story that's not mine to tell. The whole town can breath a sigh of relief that Mr. Morton is dead but an even deeper sigh because one of our own didn't kill him. Although, now we're still left with the possibility that someone is a jewel thief."

"Yes, as to that," began Alice, "Mrs. Clarendon definitely knew Margery Somerville and her father. What I don't think she knows is how much she actually revealed. When I was talking about Gladys and, I'm sorry, Aunt Dorothea, your lack of character discernment, she commented that Margery Somerville might be good at disguises but not that good."

"So … without you specifically pointing out to her that Gladys was in fact Margery, she segued directly from Gladys to Margery and Margery's ability with disguises or aliases if you will. I think it isn't too much of a stretch to make the assumption that Margery has used aliases before and that Fiona knew that," mused Dorothea.

"Exactly," said Edith. "She also mentioned that Bertram and Margery joined a dig in Egypt."

"Did she say when?"

"Some years after the war," replied Alice.

"Well, then. Has Margery been in contact over the years with Fiona and does that mean that Fiona has the brooch?" mused Dorothea.

"But how on earth would they know I would have it or for that matter that I would be here?" queried Edith.

"My telegram about the Guy Fawkes party?" reminded Dorothea.

"Ahhh yes. When I pictured the evening again you were absolutely right to ask about it."

"What do you mean?" asked Alice.

"Margery Somerville was at the ball when I was there," explained Edith. "One of those faces seen in the background. That's why I always felt that 'Gladys Cooper' looked vaguely familiar."

"And?" Alice looked quizzically at Dorothea.

Dorothea didn't answer. She tilted her head and looked again into the fire.

"I also talked to Mary Pequegnant," she finally said.

Edith and Alice looked at each other and shrugged.

"I'm waiting to hear from Harold. He must get back to me very soon or I fear it will be too late," said Dorothea.

"What do you know?" her sister demanded.

"Nothing for an absolute certainty but it seems like pieces are starting to fit together."

"Who do you think did it?" asked Alice.

"As I said, I need to hear from Harold and also to confirm a few other details. And I should speak with Chief Goodman. I could be wrong so I don't want to disclose anything yet."

"But you don't think you're wrong, do you?" asked Edith.

Dorothea looked at her steadily.

"No, I don't think I'm wrong."

Dorothea sat at the kitchen table with Dianna.

"Dianna, I need you to think back to the morning after our guests arrived. As I recall, Mr. Seyler mentioned that Margery and Mr. MacMurray were discussing hot water bottles. Did you happen to hear their conversation?"

"Yes, Mrs. Montgomery. The night they arrived, Gladys ... Margery had filled all the hot water bottles as she always did and put them in everyone's bed. I was walking past Mr. MacMurray's room and noticed his on his chair. I thought maybe she had been called to do something and forgot to go back and put his in his bed. I went in and picked it up but it was empty so I took it downstairs and filled it and took it back up and placed it in his bed.

"The next morning, I heard Mr. MacMurray say, 'I thought you said you took care of the hot water bottles.' And Gla ... Margery said, "I did. I had no idea she would notice it.' And he said, 'Well, it's still wet and swollen and it's stuck so I'll have to wait until it dries.' It seemed a strange thing to say."

"Very good, my dear. Can you think of any other time you heard them talking together?"

"Well that first evening"

Dorothea nodded. "We played cards."

"When everyone went home, Margery and I were finishing up the dishes. Mr. MacMurray came into the kitchen with a sherry glass. 'You missed this one,' he said. Margery asked me to go and see if there were others that hadn't been picked up. As I left, I heard him say, 'Someone named Mary Pequegnant is a jewel expert. She might spot it.' And that's all."

"Thank you, Dianna. They didn't mention anyone else from town?"

"Not that I heard."

"It's an unpleasant business; you've been most helpful."

Chapter 21: Outfoxed

The next evening saw the gathering of a dinner party at the home of Eleanor and Chester Smith. The invitees were Elizabeth and David Foxe and Ewan MacMurray along with Margery Somerville. The mock turtle soup had just been cleared away and the Waldorf salad put in its place.

"So, Ewan, you set out for England tomorrow, is that right?" asked Chester.

"I do indeed."

"Has it been an enriching trip for you; seeing old friends and making new?" enquired Eleanor.

"It has. I owe a debt of gratitude to my old friends for connecting me with my new," he said, smiling and raising his wine glass toward the Foxes and then to Chester and Eleanor.

"It's been our gain," replied Eleanor, raising her glass in response.

"And a bonus for us to be introduced to your charming companion," said Chester, smiling and nodding at Margery.

"The question being, of course, is Margery an old or new friend," continued Eleanor in a teasing tone.

"A bit of both, eh, my dear," said Elizabeth Foxe.

"Indeed," replied Margery with a touch of coolness.

"This is such a grand home but surely not very old," interposed Ewan.

"In its merest infancy compared to your houses," said Chester. "Our father, early in life, was very successful in business and built this for his ladylove, our mother."

"He was in banking, was he not?" asked David Foxe.

"Yes and electricity."

"And you follow in his footsteps?" asked Margery.

"I do but I've also branched out."

"Oh?"

In removing a salad plate, their server fumbled and let it fall with a thud onto the carpet.

"Please excuse, Winston," said Eleanor, "he's new to the job. Thank you, Winston."

"You've branched out you say," prompted Elizabeth Foxe.

"Yes." Chester paused, waiting for Winston to remove the remaining plates and leave the room.

"I have branched into what could be called 'exports and imports'," he replied meaningfully.

"Ah," murmured David Foxe knowingly.

The guests visibly relaxed and everyone smiled expansively at one another.

"This item of interest you mentioned in your invitation, does it have anything to do with your 'exports and imports'?" asked Ewan.

"As a matter of fact, it does." Chester lowered his voice slightly. "I have a contact in Egypt who is in a position to, shall we say, edit the contents of archaeological digs. He chooses small pieces he thinks will sell well as jewelry. The piece is copied using, ahem, less than precious gems but sold privately as a unique find straight from a dig. At the same time, the original is sold along with other items from the collection to the highest bidding museum. It's risky but the likelihood of someone from here traveling to an Egyptian museum is extremely low and therefore worth the risk. We've been highly successful. Unfortunately we've recently hit a snag."

A pause as Winston and another server lay out various steaming bowls of Chinese entrees. A third server filled the wine glasses. When they withdrew Chester continued.

"Our paste replicas are created in Edinburgh but our man there has just died."

"Who was he?" asked Ewan.

"What his real name was we never knew. He went by Mr. McGoo," replied Eleanor.

Margery looked searchingly at Eleanor but her face was blandly serious.

"How is this of interest to us?" asked Ewan.

"The way you handled the Willowsdown affair was inspiring and we thought you might be able to help us find another, mmm, replica artist," said Eleanor.

"I'm taking a supreme risk here," said Chester, "but hear me out. My guess is that you, Ewan, took the original from your father's dig and had it copied using the skills of the Foxes here. Margery was planted in Willowsdown in order to make the switch. Please forgive my broad strokes in what was surely a finely tuned enterprise."

The four guests exchanged wary glances.

"My proposal" continued Chester, "is that having lost our 'replica artist,' we could use the expertise of people right on our doorstep," he said, nodding to Elizabeth and David, "and perhaps retain in some manner the architect of the Willowsdown transaction?" he said questioningly to Ewan.

"I was the architect," said Margery quietly. "He was the assistant."

"I would like," said Ewan slowly, "to see this item of interest you have spoken of, but first I'd like to know how it is that you linked us with Mrs. Heyer's beetle brooch?"

"Ah, yes," began Chester.

Winston and the two other servers appeared in the room.

"Actually, I wasn't the one who did the linking. Winston, if you'd be so kind as to take over from here."

Ewan jumped to his feet, the melting brown eyes Dorothea had admired on meeting him hardened into flint.

"You've set us up," he snarled.

"No!" cried Margery who pushed her chair back hard against the serving fellow standing behind her.

"Now miss, don't make it worse for yourself by resisting arrest." So said Constable Thompson who, along with his compatriot and his supervisor, Senior Constable Winston Hutchison, had been acting as wait staff in readiness for the springing of the trap.

"You've brought this on us! You've done this!" shouted David Foxe, pointing at Margery and Ewan. "Those people from Willowsdown! I knew they were fishy!"

"Now, now," said Senior Constable Hutchison. "The less said the better. This is an international affair but we'll start by taking you to the station. I'm sorry about this, ma'am, but I need your wrists for the handcuffs."

At which point, Elizabeth Foxe, who had been sitting pale and frozen, slid from her seat in a dead faint.

Mrs. Foxe was revived and the troop was bundled into various police vehicles. Chester and Eleanor retreated to the kitchen, a favorite spot from childhood.

"Mrs. McCluskey, I'm afraid your scrumptious upside down cake will not dazzle anyone besides ourselves," said Chester, slumping into a chair.

"You'll be proud to know that your wee bairns wheeled in the bad guys," grinned Eleanor.

"Weel now, isnae tha' gran'. Ye just set thaur an' I'll be getting' the cake an' some tea an' ye can teel me all abit it."

"But first," said Eleanor, "we really must call Mrs. Montgomery and tell her that she was right."

After receiving a jubilant account from Eleanor, Dorothea also took a call from Chief Goodman.

"The police searched their rooms and found Mrs. Heyer's brooch stitched into the lining of one of Mr. MacMurray's jackets. I'll be sending Joe North first shot tomorrow morning to fetch it and drop it round as soon as he's back in town," said a buoyant Chief Goodman.

"And the matching piece?" asked Dorothea.

"Likely in London. Evidently Mr. MacMurray isn't cooperating on that front but we'll get it in the end."

"And Fiona Clarendon didn't play a part in this."

"Seems she's not implicated in this at all."

"Not in this one anyway."

"Now, Mrs. Montgomery ..."

"Yes, yes. I'll let sleeping dogs lie."

"Glad to hear it. But I would like to know how you noodled out this case."

"Oh Chief, I'm too tired and relieved and exhilarated to give you a sensible account. When you drop by with Edith's brooch, plan to stay and I'll tell you everything. But let me thank you again for trusting my judgment and taking my suppositions seriously and for making all the subsequent arrangements."

"Well, police work isn't all by the rule book. There's a good bit to be said for common sense and character judgment not to mention a good dose of understandin' the workings of the human heart."

"Amen to that," said Dorothea laughing. "Thanks for the call and a good night to you."

Chapter 22: Unearthing the Beetle

The following afternoon found Edith proudly wearing her returned brooch.

"I'm keeping the copy. I'll wear it whilst careening through large parties and any thievery minded person is welcome to snatch it," she had told Dorothea the night before.

Now the household, along with Chief Goodman, settled in the front sitting room to hear Dorothea's account.

"Well?" prodded Edith. "When you told Alice and me the other day you thought you knew who stole the brooch, were you correct? Had you known all along? Surely not."

"Yes, that day my surmises were proven to be right, but no, I didn't know all along. I'm ashamed to say I allowed unworthy thoughts to hover about a great many entirely innocent people."

"You didn't suspect me, did you, old bean?" asked George grinning impishly.

"Old bean! George! Really!" admonished his grandmother.

"You should know by now, Edith, he just does it to get your goat," said Charles dryly.

"Hmph," muttered Edith. "I suppose everyone at the Livingstone party was suspect."

"Well, yes," admitted Dorothea, "I knew Isaac Kingswood had passed by the chair where the scarf with the brooch was draped and I knew he needed money in order to be taken seriously by Olive's father.

And Violet was sitting practically right on it and then flitted off to Toronto the next day."

"And Dr. Withrow and his wife left town abruptly," offered Edith.

"And the Merriweather sisters suddenly were able to afford insurance," observed Charles.

"Then, of course, my suspicions of Chamberlain Johnson, having heard about this money he was expecting," Dorothea commented.

"As you said at the time, I had lost something precious and the folk of Willowsdown had lost trust," said Edith.

"Yes," sighed Dorothea. "I was quite certain that none of these people could have taken it but there is always a niggling doubt—we none of us know how we will respond in the face of a particular temptation. What if someone was overtaken by the moment? Everywhere I looked it seemed there were plausible motives. I would like to point out though that it never crossed my mind to link either you, Betty and Dilman, or you, Dianna, to the theft."

Dianna blushed and said, "Thank you, Mrs. Montgomery."

Dilman sat up taller in his seat and Betty, dabbing her eyes with her handkerchief, blurted out, "Well, and I'm not seeing how you ever could!"

"But you suspected Margery?" asked Alice.

"Not until the discovery of the jars of broth."

"Right," said Chief Goodman, "the jars of broth. How did that set off your train of thought? No pun intended."

"Since only the jars and not the basket were tossed from the train, it meant that it wasn't simply a very odd accident. It seemed to me they must have been deliberately thrown out. Had she thrown them out or had someone else? But why and if someone else, who?

Was she safe? I remembered she hadn't left a forwarding address and that made me wonder if it was really an oversight or had it been intentional? The whole scenario seemed odd enough to make it worth looking into further. Knowing Reverend Watkins to be someone who has contacts far and wide, I showed him that Christmas picture. My thinking was that if there was a way to track her then I could know she was safe and the whole jar episode could be put down to an abhorrence of beef stock. But, of course, Reverend Watkins knew our Gladys Cooper as Margery Somerville, daughter of Bertram Somerville."

Edith nodded. "The fellow who sold the brooch to Harold."

"To me," said Dorothea, "a false identity generally means someone is hiding for safety or hiding for more sinister reasons. So it was time to do some digging."

"When Grandmama and I were at Mrs. Clarendon's," said Alice slowly, "she told us that Margery and her father had joined a dig in Egypt. That must have been Ewan's father's dig!"

"Exactly so, my dear," said Dorothea. "I cabled Harold and asked him to discover the exact connection of Margery and her father to the dig. It turns out that after the two beetle brooches had been excavated, one needed repairs. Some gems needed to be replaced or some such thing. Harold was unsure of the details but no matter; the fact is that they were separated. The one needing repairs was lost by a careless curator's assistant but then found by Bertram Somerville when he joined the dig. But I'm getting ahead of myself.

"Once Margery was placed at an archaeological dig in Egypt I realized it was highly probable there was a connection between Margery and Ewan. I noted that Margery had only been in my employ since mid-November and at the time I thought she was an unlikely candidate for domestic service. What if she and Ewan had long planned this and she had been sent over? Again, all very imaginative but not impossible.

"Do you remember the morning after your arrival?" she asked, directing her question to Alice and George, "the two of you and Ewan walked downtown and on arrival back home, you told me Ewan was having a word with 'Gladys' about hot water bottles?"

The sister and brother puckered their brows in remembrance.

"Oh yes!" said Alice. "George was making comments about the 'dolls' at the phone exchange office."

George's face flushed.

"That evening" said Dorothea, "Ewan told me his friends were over their illness but hoped he could stay a day or two longer anyway. At the time I thought it was for your sake, Alice."

Alice looked sober. Edith, sitting in the chair beside her granddaughter, squeezed her arm.

"Wasn't it?" asked Charles.

"No. I put the two scenes together from the perspective that Margery and Ewan were in league. Dianna, tell Chief Goodman what you heard the morning of the hot water bottle discussion."

"Mr. MacMurray said, 'I thought you said you took care of the water bottles.' Then Margery said, 'I do. I had no idea she would notice it.' And then he said, 'Well, it's still wet and swollen and it's stuck so I'll have to wait until it dries.'"

Dorothea continued, "Dianna told me that she had noticed that Ewan's hot water bottle was lying on a chair. She knew Margery had already filled the other bottles and placed them in the various beds so she reasoned Margery had been waylaid and forgotten this one. Is that right, dear?"

Dianna nodded.

"I surmised that while unpacking Edith's things, Margery stole the pin, switched it with the paste replica and placed it in a small sack in Ewan's hot water bottle. When Dianna filled it, she soaked the sack inside causing it to swell so that it could not be removed. This meant that Ewan would have to wait until the sack dried before he could remove himself and the brooch from the house. To me that explained the water bottle conversation between Margery and Ewan. And the very odd squealy, gaspy sound I heard early in the morning of Ewan's departure. He had finally been able remove the sack with the brooch in it from the water bottle."

"But what about the fake?" asked George. "How does that fit in? And what about our jaunt to Toronto?"

"Well, that has to do with the second exchange that Dianna overheard."

"Which was?" asked Charles.

Dorothea nodded to Dianna.

"Margery and I was washing up and Mr. MacMurray came in and whispered to her, 'Someone named Mary Pequegnant is a jewel expert. She might spot it.'"

"They weren't counting on someone in little old Willowsdown having an expert eye," inserted Chief Goodman.

Charles chuckled. "I bet that evening when we were discussing Mary Pequegnant's expert eye for gems set them on edge."

Dorothea nodded. "Once I began thinking about connections between Margery and Ewan, I remembered that incident. Ewan had found a sherry glass that had not been collected and took it to the kitchen himself. Nothing very noteworthy except in the context of the conversation he had just heard. If, in their midst, there was someone proficient in gems, then Margery should be alerted. The fear being, of course, that the phony brooch would be spotted once Edith began to wear it. As we all know now, Ewan was long gone before Mary discovered the fake in the folds of Edith's hand bag and so who would ever link him with the theft?"

"From their statements we know for a certainty that Mrs. Montgomery's surmises were right," said Chief Goodman. "Margery switched the pins while she was unpacking your things, Mrs. Heyer, planting the real brooch in the hot water bottle. The back story, again from their statements, is that Margery and her father joined Mr. MacMurray's dig shortly before Ewan did. By that time the beetle brooches had been excavated and separated in order for the one to be repaired. Ewan, unaware that there were two brooches, stole the one that was still at the site. In the meantime, he learned there was a matching one that was lost. When the brooch was found by Mr. Somerville, Ewan's father gifted it to him. In the meantime, according to sources connected through your husband, Mrs. Heyer, Mr. MacMurray and his son had a falling out. Between that and a serious illness, Mr. MacMurray retired from the field. He had no knowledge that his son was a thief."

"So now Ewan had one brooch and Margery's father the other," continued Dorothea. "Mr. Somerville subsequently sells it to Harold and dies about a year later. Obviously, the pair is worth more together so Margery and Ewan await their opportunity. It comes on November 5 at the Guy Fawkes party. When I asked Edith to think back carefully to the faces at the party she remembered seeing Margery."

"Only very briefly," said Edith, "but when I saw her here she seemed familiar. Of course, a face seen at a ball in London would hardly be expected to be seen as a housemaid in Canada. Context is everything."

"So then Charles checked for me with his ocean liner connections and, sure enough, a Margery Somerville sailed from Southampton, England on November 7. Margery admits to shadowing Edith at the Guy Fawkes party and overhearing her tell a friend that she was coming to Canada as well as all the details of who, what, when, where, and why."

"Heavens," exclaimed Edith throwing up her hands. "One can't carry on a simple chat with a friend without it becoming grist for someone's mill."

"Margery is sent posthaste with the stolen beetle brooch to Elizabeth and David Foxe: a couple with whom Ewan has already had dealings.

"The plan is that they make a copy while she finds employment in our household. Upon asking at the post office, I learned that while in Willowsdown, Margery received one telegram. When I thought about it, I remembered that usually on her days off she stayed around town but there was one day that she took the train out. The telegram had been from Elizabeth Foxe saying the paste brooch was ready."

"And Ewan?" asked Alice.

"Ewan, meantime, knew when you were sailing. So he sailed with you and made himself agreeable, concocting a story of sick friends so that he could stay with us. He couldn't know for certain that Edith brought the pin but obviously that is what he and Margery were counting on."

"But he would have known for certain early on because, Grandmama, you wore the pin that one night at the captain's table," observed Alice.

"So how do the Smiths fit in and what did you mean when you said you got more than expected at the Foxes' jewelry store?" queried George.

"Yes! That was such a bolt from heaven. I had a vague memory of Mary Pequegnant's father apprenticing a young man in the jewelry business who subsequently moved to Toronto. On a hunch, I sent her a telegram asking if that young man's name was David Foxe. It was. It didn't move me forward in any way until we saw, at the Foxes' jewelry store, the monarch brooch: a brooch in the shape of the coronation crown. David Foxe claimed to have uniquely created it in 1920."

"He didn't?" asked George.

Dorothea shook her head.

"What I knew, and he did not know I knew, was that at Pequegnants' Jewelry there is a one of a kind piece crafted by Mary's father years ago just about the time that David Foxe was an apprentice. And the piece made by David Foxe looks exactly the same. Proof that he was a copycat."

George whistled. "Caught red handed."

"And Violet's friends, the Smiths? George said they seemed uneasy at you being there," remarked Alice.

"They were. They thought we were a delegation, so to speak, coming to scold them about wooing Violet to the big city. Rather naïve and funny actually. Before you came down for breakfast, George, I cleared the air and explained why we were really there. I took a chance on taking them into my confidence, but by then I was almost positive I had the thing worked out. As far as I could see, they played no part in the theft. Again I had had my sad suspicions of them: it felt good to lay them aside!

"Once I received Harold's cable with at least the bare facts of the two pins and the Somerville and MacMurray connection, I confided the details I knew as fact and the details I was surmising to Chief Goodman. I asked him to put it all before the Toronto constabulary along with my plan for a dinner party."

"Which worked like a charm. Far better than anyone supposed, I must admit," said the chief frankly.

"So," said Edith slowly, "had the phony brooch not been lost in that tear in the lining of my handbag, I never would have known that a switch had been made; at least not until Margery and Ewan were long out of the country. Well, thankfully no one in Willowsdown was actually tempted to steal that pin as that person would have found himself with a pile of putty on his hands; hardly worth the effort and shame."

"I'll have to make you an honorary member of the police force, Mrs. Montgomery. Can't say for sure that I'd have worked it out," admitted the chief.

Dorothea glanced fondly at each one in the room, "I think," she said, 'this is what's called teamwork."

Chapter 23: All As it Should Be

"Let's have a party!" blurted Edith. "A lost-and-found-it's-a-new-year-and-surely-spring-will-come-some-day party and invite all the people you suspected."

"As did you!" rejoined Dorothea, raising her brows and tilting her head.

"Indeed."

With all the flurry of the final days of the year, the Montgomery household had spent a quiet New Year's Eve and a tranquil few weeks. They were now heading into the last half of January. Although when the sun rose it still sparkled up a snowy landscape, "the poorest twig on the elm-tree was ridged inch deep with pearl", its rays shone just a little longer each day; a sign that the long dark would give way.

"I know I said that I wanted to experience a Canadian winter but really enough is enough. Does spring ever arrive?"

"We live by faith not by sight," teased Dorothea. "Of course, it does and it's all the more precious for the wait. Now this party …"

"Welcome, welcome," announced Charles heartily. "Just go right back to the kitchen, Mrs. Withrow. Mrs. White will be glad for the extra cream. Fresh from the farm I suppose."

Dr. Withrow winked.

"One of the best ways to get paid."

"So exceedingly beneficent of you to invite us. An English high tea how ... how," stammered Mrs. Johnson unexpectedly lost for words.

" ... delightful," finished Mr. Johnson.

"It seemed fitting as Edith is leaving next week," said Dorothea, hanging their coats on an extra hall tree made available for the occasion.

Violet was home for the weekend so the Readers' Club, all except George and Elva North who were sitting together on the other side of the room, were gathered together in a corner with plates piled with sandwiches and scones and dainties.

Suddenly a whoop and clapping broke from the club.

"Hear, hear," called Nelson Jr. "Someone has an announcement."

Olive Robertson rose from her chair as Isaac Kingswood took her hand to stand up with him.

"I," Isaac cleared his throat. "I would like to say that Olive and I are getting married in June."

Whistles from George, many oohs and aahs from Willowsdown's matrons and overall applause.

"Did you already know?" Dorothea asked Eleanor and Chester Smith when the hubbub subsided.

"Yes," replied Eleanor. "He said he was tired of waiting for Uncle's unreasonable approval so he went ahead and asked Olive and is letting the chips fall where they may. I'm very happy for them."

"There you are," said Edith as she joined the trio.

"I see you're wearing *the* pin," commented Chester.

"How could I not? Let me say again how thankful I am for the role you played in its retrieval."

Edwina swooped by.

"Mary and I were saying that this should become an annual event and maybe include the Girl Guides or have a separate event for them and the Women's Institute, or ... hello, Dorothea." Edwina drew a quick

breath as she bussed Dorothea on both cheeks. "Sorry
I'm late. The neighbor's baby was fussing, fussing,
fussing, poor thing and she was frantic so I went over
and helped out and then caught my finger in the door
jam as I was leaving so went home and iced it. What a
lovely thing!" Here she was referring to the table's
centerpiece not the injured and iced finger.

Annie Hacker, the Merriweather sisters, and Mr. and
Mrs. Wainfleet were in deep conversation, balancing
tea cups on their laps as were George and Elva North.
The tete-a-tete between the latter, however, had an
entirely different look to it than the chatter taking place
amongst the group of old friends.

"I'm going to miss Willowsdown so much," said
Alice to Dorothea as she smeared jam and cream on a
scone.

"Willowsdown will miss you. You've made good
friends here. And Edith assures me that the loss of
Ewan didn't cut too deeply."

"Not at all. A wee heartbreak is likely good for the
soul. Some heartbreak alongside the gathering in of
new friends makes a poignant combination. It makes
the place where it all happened very special. I'm hoping
that my next place will be as notable."

Alice looked at Dorothea with a gleam in her eye.

"And that place being?"

"Oxford. I'm going to apply to Somerville College."

"Oh, my dear. I couldn't ask for anything more
perfect for you! Edith must be so pleased."

"I must say she is," agreed Alice beaming.

"Your great grandmother would be bursting with
pride, and very envious, if she knew you are to be a
university student. By all accounts she was smart as a
whip as are you."

"Thank you. My academic ambitions have been stirring for awhile but this time with you has cemented them."

"In what way?"

"I can't say for sure but I fancy it was observing you putting your mind to work that was the final impetus. I realized how much I relish learning and contemplating and analyzing and where better to strive for excellence in that than at Oxford?"

"You will do well. It seems that all that has transpired had more layers of meaning than we could ever have imagined. There's some philosophy for you," said Dorothea winking.

"So," began Dorothea to Charles as they sat together for a moment observing their guests. "My guess is that our bonny Elva North will be the wearer of those earrings George bought at Foxes' Jewels."

His sandwich stopping halfway to his mouth, Charles stared at her. He slowly continued the ascent of the sandwich and took a bite without removing his eyes from her.

"You do beat all," he finally said.

THE END

ABOUT THE AUTHOR

Elizabeth Jukes has always enjoyed reading. Often, as a child, she would hold up a book to the slice of light from the front porch lamp that the not quite closed bedroom curtain allowed in. All this, of course, when she was supposed to be asleep.

Love of reading translated to love of writing. A Journalism Diploma followed, as well as a Bachelor of Theology, and then, with life's twists, many years of no writing except for journaling. But a few years ago, the Dorothea Montgomery character and Dorothea's town of Willowsdown appeared in her mind and the desire to flesh that all out in *Pin It on a Dead Man* was irresistible. She hopes this book and ones to come will tempt people to read beyond their bedtimes.

Elizabeth lives in New Hamburg, Ontario with her husband, Jon, and their two sons.

Proof

Made in the USA
Columbia, SC
10 March 2018